Just ahead of them, the block teemed with hundreds of zombies. They drifted drowsily, like crazed sleepwalkers.

"Sick. . . ." Madison shuddered.

"Sick!" Rice smiled.

A teenage zombie wearing a BurgerDog polo shirt and server's cap turned to face them. His left knee buckled backward, and he tottered with an excruciating sidelong limp. His head tilted to the right where the side of his neck was missing a large hunk. The drive-through headset and microphone were still clamped to his head.

Zack did not want fries with that.

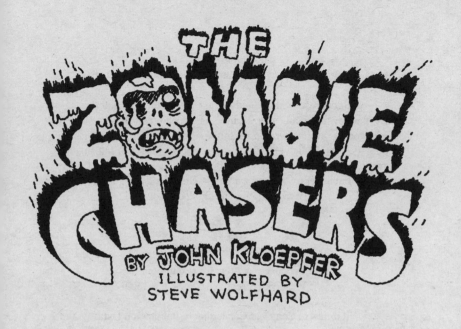

THE ZOMBIE CHASERS

BY JOHN KLOEPFER

ILLUSTRATED BY STEVE WOLFHARD

HARPER

An Imprint of HarperCollinsPublishers

The Zombie Chasers
Copyright © 2010 by Alloy Entertainment and John Kloepfer

Produced by Alloy Entertainment
151 West 26th Street, New York, NY 10001

Library of Congress Cataloging-in-Publication Data
Kloepfer, John.
The zombie chasers / John Kloepfer ; illustrations by Steve
Wolfhard. — 1st ed.
          p.   cm.
Summary: When zombies take over Phoenix, Arizona, Zack Clarke,
his best friend, Rice, and his older sister's mean friend Madison Miller
team up to try to defeat the undead, or at least survive one another.
ISBN 978-0-06-185306-7
[1. Zombies—Fiction.   2. Survival—Fiction.   3. Phoenix (Ariz.)—
Fiction.   4. Horror stories.]   I. Wolfhard, Steve, ill.   II. Title.
PZ7.K8646Zom   2010   2010004602
[Fic]—dc22   CIP
                                                          AC

Design by Andrea C. Uva
13 14 15   CG/BR   20 19 18 17 16 15 14 13
❖
First paperback edition, 2011

For Abigail —J. K.

To my mom and dad
for their love and patience —S. W.

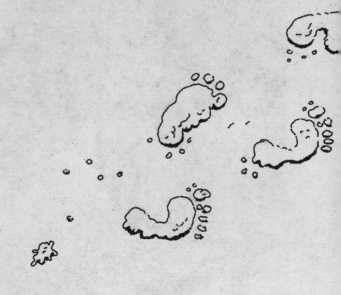

CHAPTER

Dusk settled over the neighborhood. The humid air was thick as pulp.

Zack Clarke turned onto Locust Lane after a slow walk home, expecting the usual Friday night action on his block: the Zimmer twins grinding out tricks on their skateboards across the parkway; Mrs. Mansfield coming home from the video store with bags of fast food and DVDs for her lazy children; or Old Man Stratton prowling the sidewalks, a disintegrating paperback clutched in his veiny hand. But on this muggy Arizona evening, there wasn't a soul to be seen.

Hunched down under the weight of his backpack,

Zack quickened his pace, eager to get home. Earlier in the day, a food fight had landed him in after-school work detention, polishing his middle school's linoleum floors. Now all Zack wanted was the one leftover slice of chocolate birthday cake waiting in the refrigerator, wrapped in plastic and tagged with a Post-it: ZACK'S B-DAY CAKE, DO NOT TOUCH!

Zack could see his house now, his mom's Volvo station wagon sitting in the driveway. Every light in the house was off—all except the one in his sister's bedroom above the garage. He watched from the sidewalk

as Zoe's room went dark, leaving the house looking empty and deserted.

But Zack knew that his older sister, Zoe, and her evil trio of eighth-grade she-devils—Madison Miller, Ryan York, and Samantha Donovan—were having one of their notorious sleepovers at his house. So until Mom and Dad returned from parent-teacher night at his school, it would just be him. And them.

As he reached the stoop, a street lamp flickered and went dead, casting the entire lawn in shadow. He pushed the front door open slowly. "Hello!" he called out into the darkness. "Zoe?"

Suddenly, the door slammed shut, and he felt a paper bag crinkle down over his head. A voice shouted, "Gotcha!"

In an instant, four pairs of hands grabbed Zack by his elbows and ankles, hoisted him off the ground, and began to carry him through the foyer. Caught in their monster-tight grip, Zack squirmed uselessly, unable to twist free.

His captors plopped him down hard on an old

wooden desk chair, the bag still over his head. Someone was holding his wrists behind the chair, bending his arms back as if he were a handcuffed prisoner. He writhed and kicked, trying to buck loose. Frustrated and exhausted, Zack went limp, playing possum for a second, before thrashing wildly in one final burst of energy.

That's when he heard a digital beep, and someone lifted the bag off his head. His sister, Zoe, stood before him. Directly behind her, their father's laptop sat open on the coffee table, and Zack could see himself on the computer screen.

"Zoe, what are you doing? You know Dad doesn't let us play with the webcam."

"I'm not playing, little brother," she said, flipping her dark hair back and cocking her head all too glamorously, like America's Next Top Psycho preparing for her closeup. "I'm producing a new reality show for VH1. It's called *Hostage Makeover*. You want to be in it?" A sinister grin stretched across her face.

"I'd rather die in my own vomit," Zack answered.

"Tough luck, kiddo," Zoe snickered. "Look alive, girls!"

Samantha and Ryan entered the living room and shimmied behind Zack. Ryan held a giant roll of duct tape in one hand, and when Zack turned around, she tucked it behind her back. "No peeking, young Zachariah!" she chided, patting him on the head.

"Okay, Zacky, you hold still!" Zoe gestured to her two minions. A second later, Ryan and Samantha were circling Zack, taping his upper arms and shoulders firmly to the back of the chair, quickly moving on to his legs until they were sure he couldn't escape. The

mysterious pair of hands behind him finally unclasped his wrists. Zack felt the blood rush, throbbing in his fingertips.

Again, he tried to wriggle free, but the tape was too strong.

Zoe adjusted the webcam to capture her brother's struggle. Then she crouched down in front of the computer and spoke: "Welcome to the premiere of *Hostage Makeover.* I am your host, Zoe Clarke. You've already met our captive, my unfortunate-looking younger brother, Zachary Arbutus Clarke." She stepped away from the laptop. "Tell us how you're feeling, Hostage Boy."

"Zoe, seriously, lay off." Zack said.

"Zoe, seriously, lay off," a voice mimicked him.

Madison Miller emerged from behind the chair, holding a polka-dotted makeup case. Madison was the prettiest girl in school, with long, almost blond, light brown hair, and just a few faint freckles dotting her button nose. She was also one of the tallest girls in the eighth grade, and she towered over Zack, gazing down at him with her big blue eyes.

"Shut up, Madison. No one's talking to you."

"*Shut up, Madison. No one's talking to you,*" Madison continued in her baby voice.

"Stop copying me," Zack insisted.

"*Stop copying me.*" Madison wouldn't quit.

"I'm an idiot," Zack said, trying to outsmart her.

"Yes, Zachary, I'm afraid you are."

Game over.

Madison opened up the makeup case and pulled out what looked like colored pencils. Then she took a sip of her favorite drink, kiwi-strawberry VitalVeganPowerPunch.

"You know, Madison," Zack said. "I heard something, that if you drink too much of that stuff it can, like, mess with your whole biological makeup."

"Did someone say 'makeup'?" Zoe chirped.

With that, Madison pulled out a frightening array of cosmetics and placed them on the coffee table. Zack had no idea what all this stuff was used for, other than cluttering up Zoe's bathroom.

"Listen up, little bro." Zoe formed a little rectangle with her index fingers and thumbs and peered through it like some kind of Hollywood director. "If you play nice, we're gonna make you look really, really pretty. But if you disturb me while I'm filming, we will make you look silly, then I will lock you in your room, put this video on YouTube, and email the link to everyone at school. Now be a good hostage."

"Zoe, let me go or I'll tell Mom and Dad that you've been sneaking out of the house at night," Zack blurted in desperation.

"Oh, dear brother," Zoe sneered. "Good hostages don't make threats."

She hit the space bar and yelled, "Action!"

CHAPTER

Zack should have been a better hostage.

He stared at his reflection in the bedroom window. Zoe had kept her promise. The girls had made him look quite silly indeed, and now Zack was a prisoner in his own home.

Madison had smeared his mouth with bright red-orange lipstick, while Samantha had caked his eyelids with silvery blue powder. Ryan sopped his hair from behind with gobs of mega-hold super-gel, styling seven spikes around his head like the Statue of Liberty. He looked like a deranged circus clown. *Zoe has to pay for this,* he thought. But before he could get any sort of revenge, Zack had to escape his locked bedroom and wash this horror show off his face.

And after all he'd been through today, he wanted that cake now more than ever.

Zack kneeled in front of the window and stared out over the neighborhood. Without his laptop or his cell phone—both of which Zoe had confiscated before locking him inside—it was the only way he could think of to pass the time. He found some comfort in watching without being seen, observing things from a distance.

There was a word for this feeling, but he couldn't come up with it. He just gazed down onto the deserted Friday night street, waiting for something to happen, desperately hoping for anyone, anything upon which to spy. But Locust Lane was dead still. Nobody around.

Zack wandered across the room to

check on his much-neglected ant farm. He couldn't remember the last time he'd actually fed them—weeks ago, maybe months. Most of the ants had starved, and the ones still struggling to survive fought vigorously over the shiny black carcasses, ripping off legs from thoraxes. Zack thought about feeding them now, but he couldn't even remember where he'd put their pellets. Probably in the back of the closet, he figured, along with everything else.

And then it struck him.

He threw open the closet door and crawled past piles of comic books and shoe boxes packed full of old *DragonBall Z* cards, way too embarrassing to play with, but way too good to throw out. A tiny dog bark sounded through the back wall of the closet. It was Twinkles, Madison's new puppy. Twinkles had had an accident on the carpet, and Zoe had banished the little dog to her bedroom. Just like Zack was to his.

Zack reached deep into the

closet, his hand landing on the case of Poland Spring water that his over-prepared mom had stashed back there for reasons unknown. Stuffed between the water and a yellow Wiffle ball bat was a rolled-up rope ladder: the key element in his dad's emergency fire-escape strategy. If being held prisoner and left to starve wasn't an emergency, then Zack didn't know what was. So he pried out a few waters from the pack and snagged the rope ladder, crawling backward into the bedroom.

Zack dumped a bottle of water over his head and scrubbed the makeup off with the slightly ripe-smelling towel balled up on the floor. Sitting on the bed now, he noticed the cordless phone sticking out from beneath his rumpled Transformers bedspread.

He grabbed the phone from under the covers and dialed. Three long rings and his best friend answered.

"Rice residence. Rice speaking."

"Yo, dude, it's me," Zack said.

"What's the word, nerd?"

"How's the plague?" Zack shuddered, thinking about

the pink crispy scabs caked in dried amber pus all over Rice's body. He'd been out of school all week with chicken pox.

"Itchy, man," Rice replied. "Real itchy."

"Well, at least Zoe didn't tie you up and give you a makeover."

"Dude, I saw it on YouTube! You're, like, famous. Your voice sounds kind of whiny on video, though. . . ."

"I know you're not supposed to hate your own family," Zack said, staring out the window. "But I have a hard time believing we have the same blood pumping through our veins."

"Yeah, man, Zoe's ruthless," Rice agreed. "Hey, which friends does she have over?"

"Madison Miller, Samantha Donovan, Ryan York," Zack rattled off the hit list.

"Duuuude," Rice groaned into the phone. "You have no idea how lucky you are. I want your life for just one slumber party."

"Rice, they'd eat you alive," Zack said.

"I bet they're playing Twister right now, huh?" Rice

sighed. "I'd give up chocolate to see those girls playing Twister."

"Dude! That's my sister!"

"Chill, Zack, I was just messin' around. I didn't mean Zoe, man. Madison's pretty cute, though. Not that your sis isn't cute, I mean, dude, come on . . . you know."

"I'm hanging up now!" Zack placed the phone on the desktop, opened the window, and hooked the top of the ladder to the windowsill. As he threw the bundle of tangled rope over the ledge, he heard footsteps on the sidewalk below. The figure came into view: just Old Man Stratton out for his nightly stroll. He seemed slower than usual, walking with a miserable limp. The old codger grumbled angrily to himself and disappeared into the shadows between two streetlamps.

Zack began his slow, shaky descent down the ladder, and the phone blared. He reached back through the window, clinging to the ladder with his free hand.

"Rice?" Zack answered. "I can't really talk right now."

"Dude, are you watching this?"

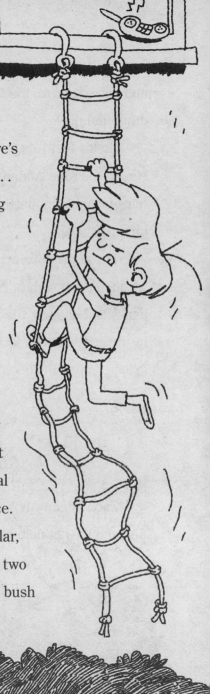

"No, actually, I'm climbing out my window."

"Don't do that, man! There's zombies, like, all over the place. . . . Hold on, hold on. They're saying how to kill them."

"Sorry, Rice," Zack said. "Gotta go." He hung up the phone and placed it flat on the windowsill. He had no time for his friend's stupid jokes.

Halfway to the ground, Zack heard something coming from the bushes below: a violent rustling, followed by a loud animal squeal. He held his breath. Silence. There was another noise, similar, but not as loud as the first, as two jackrabbits tore out from the bush and darted across the lawn. He exhaled. Just a couple of dumb bunnies.

Zack's feet hit the mulch around the front hedges. He left the rope ladder dangling and hurried around the house, each step putting him closer to his last piece of birthday cake.

The patio door off the kitchen slid open, and Zack let out a deep sigh of relief. He closed the sliding glass panel and flipped the latch to lock it in place. When he turned around, facing into the kitchen, his mouth dropped open in shock.

CHAPTER **3**

In the Clarke family kitchen, Madison Miller
was sitting in *Zack's* spot, at *Zack's* table, her
eyes closed, savoring the first bite of *Zack's* last
piece of cake.

"Yuuuummm," she exhaled in an elongated whisper.

"What are you doing?" Zack broke the silence. "That's
my triple-fudge, double-cream chocolate Oreo cake!"

"Don't you mean triple-fudge, double-*soy*-cream
chocolate Oreo cake?" Madison chewed the gooey mor-
sel slowly, taunting him from across the room.

"You know that cake's not vegan, Madison," he
informed her, reveling in this wonderful twist.

Madison and Zoe had formed a vegetarian pact last summer, which had then blossomed into a strict vegan diet. Poor Zack had been subjected to a freezer full of Rice Dream ice cream ever since.

"Right now, you're eating baby chickens and buttery cow's milk!" he continued with a mischievous smirk.

"Eeeeeewwww!" Madison let out a glass-shattering demon screech and spewed the half-chewed chocolate all over the kitchen wall. She raced over to the sink and turned on the water.

"Rinse it out real good," he teased.

But instead of putting her mouth to the faucet,

Madison picked up what was left of Zack's delicious cake, lifted it above her head, and slammed it down the drain. She hit the ON switch to the garbage disposal. The motor under the sink roared, and the cake spun violently into a watery chocolate sludge.

Madison turned to him. "Zoe said your mom *only* bakes 'animal-friendly' cakes now!" She quoted with her fingers and lowered her voice. "I'm gonna kill her."

"Well, normally she does, Madison," Zack explained. "But you see, that was *my* birthday cake. . . ." He made his way to the center of the kitchen now, rubbing his palms together slyly as he went on. "And on *my* birthday, we don't eat vegan. We eat regular."

Madison's brow furrowed with rage. "Oh, I'm sorry, was that *your* cake, Zack? Your *stupid, disgusting* cake?"

She leaned over the sink and sputtered out the remaining flecks of chocolate from the roof of her mouth. Then, reaching into her purse, she pulled out a new kiwi-strawberry VitalVeganPowerPunch and chugged back half the bottle.

"I guess it's not your fault you can't read, but it was

clearly labeled with *my* name. See?" he said holding up the plastic-wrapped note.

Madison sat down again and sipped her drink. "How'd you get out anyway, loser? And where's all your makeup? I put a lot of effort into your new look."

"I found a rope ladder. I washed my face. And I hate your guts," Zack answered.

Madison's ringtone burst into a Gym Class Heroes hook: *"Take a look at my girlfriend, girlfriend. . . ."* She took a look at herself in the cell phone, pressed TALK, and shouted into the receiver, "Greg, I told you not to call me until you're finished acting like an infant! There's no such thing as zombies." She hung up.

Zack froze. "Zombies?"

"What's the matter, Zack? Are you afraid of the boogeyman?" she taunted him, a spooky tremble in her voice.

"Who was it?" Zack demanded.

"Greg Bansal-Jones," Madison replied. "If you must know."

Oh, that Greg, Zack thought. He hated that Greg.

Suddenly, a tremendous crash shook the whole inside of the house, and they both spun toward the kitchen doorway.

"What the heck was that?" Madison shouted.

A scalp-tingling triple scream rang out from the living room. But the wild Zomanthyan shriek was cut short, replaced by an uncertain silence.

"Zoe!" Madison called.

Slow footsteps boomed across the first floor. They grew louder, shuffling closer. "Do you think it's a zombie?" Zack wondered out loud, realizing just how stupid the question sounded.

"Okay, dill weed, new rule," Madison ordered. "The next person who says the word *zombie* gets smacked upside the head, get it?"

There was another loud crash, and they could hear a faint tortured moan that rose in volume with the foot-steps.

"Where's Zoe?" Zack asked, his voice quivering.

Madison pushed past Zack and listened through the doorway. "Zoe?" She paused. "Ryan? . . . Samantha? You guys okay?" Nobody answered. "Zoe? This isn't funny. What's going on?"

A third crash interrupted the long creepy silence, followed by the low, deep-throated groan, rumbling with each unearthly gasp. They stood silently as the staggering, uneven footsteps grew louder. Zack inched closer to Madison.

"Zack, what do we do? He's coming this way!"

Suddenly, the phone blared. *Brrrrrrring!*

Startled, Zack leaped on to Madison and clung to her soft zip-up cardigan.

"Eww, dude! Not so close!" She shoved him to the

floor. He scrambled to his feet and ran to the kitchen table. *Brrrrrrring!*

"Quick, Madison! Hide!" Zack lifted up the tablecloth. Madison rolled her eyes and trotted after him. She grabbed her purse from the seat and crawled underneath the table. Zack crouched down, settling next to her in a nervous clump.

"Careful—I don't want to get nerd all over me," Madison whispered.

"Shut up, Madison." Zack jabbed her in the ribs with his elbow. She elbowed him back three times as hard. He mouthed the word *ouch* and pressed his finger to his lips for her to shush.

Brrrrrrring!

The limping shuffle grew even closer, the guttural moaning now in surround sound. The growling prowler stomped into the kitchen and stopped. The phone went silent. The intruder took heavy breaths punctuated with an abbreviated snarl.

"He sounds gross," Madison observed at full volume.

"What do we do?" Zack mouthed the words, hoping

she'd catch on. "What about Zoe?"

"I don't know," she said, a little worry in her voice.

The footsteps headed straight for the table. Madison and Zack both gulped air and held it in, exhaling silently through their nostrils. Petrified, Zack peeked under the bottom of the tablecloth, which hung only a few inches from the floor.

A pair of tattered, muck-stained sneakers and khaki pants frayed at the cuff appeared in front of his face. The legs wobbled. The sneaker soles squished and squirted as he shifted his stance, reeking like week-old cold cuts.

Madison pulled her shirt collar over her mouth.

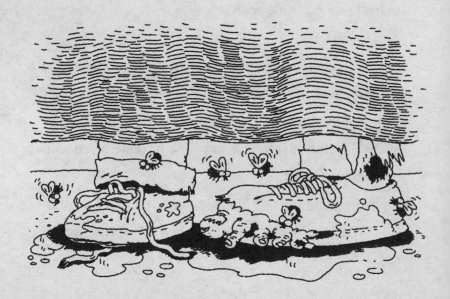

Zack's stomach churned, and he did the same. Something flapped, dropping on the linoleum with a soggy thud. Zack gasped. It was a paperback book covered in a thick dark sludge.

Old Man Stratton grunted and started wheezing in and out. He groaned and let out an awful wet cough that splatter-painted the kitchen floor with bloody red specks and gray-tinted globs of mucus. Zack shut his eyes.

Brrring! Brrring! The phone started up again.

The old man grunted once more and limped in the direction of the telephone. He grabbed the handset and ripped the cord right out of the wall, thrashing wildly. He heaved the receiver across the room, and then, whirling around, he battered into the fridge and tore the freezer door clean off. Soy ice cream thunked to the kitchen floor. A gust of cold steam obscured the man from the neck up. He reeled around, half-hunched and wild-eyed, his face deformed with massive swollen knots of flesh.

The crazy old man staggered out of the kitchen and plodded into the hallway, his footsteps fading.

"I think he's leaving," Zack whispered, his heart pounding.

Madison grabbed Zack by the arm and dragged him out from under the table. "Come on, let's get out of here."

"Wait," Zack said. "We've got to get Zoe."

"She's probably hiding somewhere. Or they got away already. Now come on!"

She pointed to the sliding glass doors, and they raced across the kitchen. Zack fumbled with the lock.

"Come on, hurry up!" Madison urged, chugging the last of her VitalVegan.

Just as he was about to slide the door open, a pale gray fist pounded against the glass, cracking it into the shape of a spiderweb. Clutched in the hand was a limp, lifeless rabbit. Madison covered her mouth, heaving a little, her eyes bugging out.

A swift wind carried a dark cloud across the moon, and the bunny squasher's silhouette came into full view. His bloody, mangled arm glistened bright red. His torn black Burton T-shirt revealed a massive chest wound, ripe with rot, and his Etnies were destroyed. The zombie teen gripped a skateboard with his other decaying hand.

"It's Danny! One of the Zimmers!" Zack exclaimed in a shocked whisper, gazing directly into his neighbor's cold, vacant eyes. Pale, sagging skin drooped from the twin's face. His jaw jutted out a bit, and his upper lip was raised, revealing his yellow incisors. Zack and Madison watched through the shattered glass as the Zimmer raised the dead bunny to his open mouth and bit into its middle, spouting blood up onto his wretched face.

"Zack, I don't know what a Zimmer is," Madison proclaimed, dumbstruck, eyes bulging, "but I think I know a zombie when I see one."

Zack paused for a second, cocked back his hand, and smacked the side of Madison's head. She glared down at him; her eyes flashed fire. Zack just shrugged.

"It was your rule," he said.

They turned around just in time to see the Zimmer twin, now a zombie twin, lifting his skateboard to smash through the door.

"Okay, no more games, Zack! Run!"

Madison and Zack whipped around and sprinted out of the kitchen and up the stairs, the crash of shattered glass echoing in their wake.

CHAPTER

Madison slammed the bedroom door behind them. Zack's forearms tightened with goose-flesh as a chilly breeze whisked through the open window. The rope ladder hung ominously off the window ledge, its rungs smacking against the side of the house. *Clack. Clack. Clack.*

Zack looked outside at the horrifying sight below: The neighborhood was alive with the undead. Zombie Samantha and zombie Ryan were ripping out clumps of each other's hair, and whole chunks of flesh had been chomped right off their necks and shoulders. Mrs. Mansfield, Old Man Stratton, the other Zimmer twin, and all the neighbors were hideously deformed, every one of them hacking up blood, gutter-logged with zombie goop, flesh bubbles bulging and then bursting. They were everywhere, covering the lawn, the sidewalk, the street, staggering aimlessly, wailing deep subhuman moans.

"Madison, get over here," Zack called.

"How do you lock this door from the inside?" she asked, jiggling the doorknob.

"You can't. Just come look at this." Zack's eyes were glued to the scene below.

Madison fished out another VitalVegan from her handbag and sidled up next to Zack. She took a casual sip, then looked out at the shambling swarm of blood-thirsty fiends. The zombies tottered randomly in every direction. Their arms were outstretched, disjointed limbs dangling out of their sockets, some slashed to shreds with bloody gashes.

Madison let out a choked yelp, dropping the plastic bottle out the window. It seemed to pause in midair before the plastic clinked noisily off the wooden slats of the ladder.

The zombies turned in unison, craning their necks toward the house.

Madison sucked in air, preparing to let out a full-fledged scream. But Zack cupped his hand over her mouth, and instead, she just sputtered into his palm. He shot her a sideways glance and wiped his hand on the side of his pants. *Gross.*

And then she screamed anyway.

The festering mob's dead milky eyes stared up at Zack and Madison. The zombies limped toward the house, converging in a slow, synchronized attack.

"Great job, Madison," Zack said sarcastically. "Just what we needed."

"Whatever, loser—" she started to say, before the phone rang again. Zack grabbed it off the windowsill and answered.

"Let me call you back, Rice," he said in a hurried whisper.

"Zack, I swear . . . if you hang up on me, you can find a new best friend," Rice threatened.

"I'm kind of in the middle of something right now."

"Yeah, Zack, you and everyone else. Your neighborhood's infested, man. The news is calling it a hot zone. I thought the zombies got you for sure."

Back at the window, Madison let out another hair-raising shriek. Zack wheeled around to look at her.

"What the heck was that?" Rice asked.

"Rice, sorry, just hold on a second. I'm not hanging up, just . . ." Zack's mouth fell open, his eyes widening as

Madison unhooked the rope ladder from the windowsill and tossed it over the ledge.

"What'd you do that for?" he asked, the phone pressed to his shoulder.

"One of them started to climb up!" she told him.

"Well, how do you expect us to get down now?"

"Did you really expect me to climb down into that . . . that . . . *zombieville*?" Madison crossed her arms and shook her head "Uh-uh, no way!"

But before Zack could respond, the cracking hinges of the front door downstairs shot a tremor that rippled up through the wall and rattled the windowpanes.

"Rice, we're in real trouble, man. What do you know about zombies?"

"Okay, Zack, first and foremost, don't get killed by the zombies. If you die, I don't really have any other pals to replace you with. So your primary objective is to stay alive and remain my best friend," he finished.

"Thanks, Rice, but seriously . . ." Zack pleaded.

"I *am* serious. So . . . just be good and don't die. Now, who else is with you?"

"Just me and Madison."

"Oh, man, you're in deep trouble," Rice said. "Have either of you been bitten? Because if you get bitten, you die and, like, your body is reanimated, but your skin starts to rot and your eyeballs fall out and sometimes you have to pick them up and put them back in your face. Oh, dude, it's so nasty—"

"Not bitten, Rice," Zack interrupted. "We just ran upstairs into my bedroom."

"You have Madison Miller in your bedroom?"

"Rice!"

"Okay, okay, just let me think for a minute." He paused. "What's she wearing?"

"Rice, c'mon, man!"

"Well?" Madison pursed her lips, losing patience.

"He's thinking." Zack shrugged.

"Give me the phone," she demanded, grabbing it off his ear. She hit the speaker button and handed it back to Zack.

"Excuse me, who am I speaking with?" Madison asked in a stern voice, pacing back and forth.

"Uh . . . this is Rice," he mumbled sheepishly.

"Well, Rice, you better tell us everything you know about these things right now, or I'm gonna turn myself into a zombie, come hunt you down, and rip your guts out, understand?"

"You can't turn your*self* into a zombie, *Madison,*" Rice said in a know-it-all tone. "Only a zombie can turn you into a zombie."

"Just lose the 'tude and tell us everything."

"Okay," Rice began, sounding a little nervous. "The first thing you have to realize about zombies is that they're just dead people who walk around and try to bite you."

Zack peered down at the carnage below. Zombies lurched across the lawn, heading toward the house. Some of them trampled through the bushes, smashing through the first-floor windows. The rest converged on the stoop, storming ravenously through the doorway. Black blood oozed out of their diseased bodies, dripping on the grass and the cobblestone walkway. Zack could hear them ransacking the first floor.

"Dude, are you listening? If they bite you, you'll get infected and become a zombie. This is what the zombies want most. That is, if they don't devour you entirely. Luckily, though, zombies are pretty slow, so it's easy to outrun them, but . . ."

Zack swiveled his head around the room, looking for something with which to defend himself. "Okay, what else, man?

Tell us everything!" He placed the phone down flat on the carpet.

"Now listen up, guys." Rice was getting serious. "You said you were upstairs in the bedroom? You have to get out of there. If you let the zombies box you into a corner like that, you're both goners."

Zack reached under his bed and pulled out a toy gun. Across the room, Madison sat on the swivel chair, looking at her reflection in a compact mirror.

"We're being attacked by walking corpses who want to eat us, and you're worried about how you look?"

Madison pursed her lips. "If I'm gonna get killed by these zombie freaks, I'm gonna go out in style." After applying lipstick, she offered some to Zack. "Wanna touch-up?"

He aimed the gun at Madison and pulled the trigger. It flashed a red laser light, bleeping a futuristic melody. Madison stuck her tongue out.

Suddenly, the unlocked door boomed and rattled. Someone-slash-thing was in the hallway, trying to pound its way into the bedroom. Madison stood up and pressed against the door with both hands, stiff-armed.

"What's going on over there?" Rice's voice sounded from the phone on the floor.

"Wuh-huh-huh . . . Rice, wh-what do I do?" Zack stuttered.

"Okay, pay attention. The only way to kill a zombie is to completely destroy its brain or chop its head off."

Zack rushed to the closet, rifling through boxes, pulling down coat hangers. Nothing. He scurried deeper past his old *DragonBall Z* cards, kicking them out of Madison's sight line. There was nothing except the thin yellow Wiffle ball bat propped in the corner.

He backed up on his hands and knees, holding the flimsy plastic club. Madison exploded with laughter.

"What? What's he doing?" Rice spoke up.

"He's got one of those plastic baseball bats," Madison scoffed. "The thing weighs like two ounces."

"Zack, get a grip," Rice scolded. "You're killing zombies, man! This is serious business. You need serious weapons."

Zack ran to his desk and started opening drawers frantically. He found a Swiss Army knife he never used and shoved it in his pocket. Then he pulled out a hammer he had forgotten to put back in his dad's toolbox and raced back to Madison.

She was bracing the door as the zombie banged relentlessly on the other side. Madison laughed abruptly, snorting through her nose.

"What's so funny?" Zack asked.

"The door's not even locked. Zombies are really stupid, huh?" Madison giggled, when suddenly the wood splintered with a menacing snap. She flinched.

"I wouldn't laugh at zombies, Madison," Rice said. "Try reading the Wikipedia entry and see if you ever sleep again."

One more thump and the wood gave way completely. The zombie's gunky onion-yellow hand shot through the door, one inch from Madison's face, reaching for something, anything, to claw.

Madison screeched, pushing herself out of the zombie's reach. Zack stood next to her, holding his weapon with both hands.

"All right, Rice, I got a hammer," he said. "Is that gonna do the trick?"

"Absolutely," Rice assured him. "When the zombie busts through, you're gonna cave that sucker's skull right in!"

Zack stood still, hammer raised over his head,

waiting. The zombie's other arm came crashing through, followed by its gruesome head. Zack nearly brought down the hammer, when he saw that this zombie was none other than his sister.

Zoe's dark, stringy hair was matted with sweat. Blue veins pulsated up through the drooping skin on her face. Her pupils were constricted to thin, black slivers of evil. She hissed and growled, scratching at the air.

"Oh my God!" Madison exclaimed. "Zoe looks really bad as a zombie!"

Zoe managed to squeeze her upper half through the hole in the door, but her legs remained out in the hallway, walking in place as though she were on a zombie treadmill.

Madison pulled out her camera phone and pointed

it at the gargling, zombified beast that her best friend had become. She laughed and clicked, chuckling a little harder with every photo.

"Hey, what's happening?" Rice said. "You kill it or what?"

"It's *Zoe*!" Zack told him.

"Dude." Rice sounded excited now. "This is what you've been waiting for your entire life!"

"I can't actually kill my sister, Rice!" Zack shouted.

"Fine. But if you're not going to kill her, you have to knock her out. Whack her on the head with something hard, right between the eyes if you can," Rice explained. "That won't kill her, though. Eventually she's going to wake up and try to get you again."

Madison shrieked then, looking through the splintered hole around Zoe's waist.

"Zack! They're coming up the stairs!"

He picked up the phone and took it off speaker. "Rice, I gotta go, man!"

"Zack, wait! After you and Madison escape, get a car, pick me up, and we'll figure things out from over here," he said. "Good luck."

"Sounds like a plan," Zack told him. "And thanks."

"Anytime, bro . . . and, dude, if I don't see you . . ." His best friend's voice took on a somber tone. A full five-second pause. "I love you, buddy." Rice hung up before Zack could respond. The dial tone buzzed in his ear.

Zack stared off into nothing, realizing for the first time that he might not make it through the night. "I love you, too, man."

"Do something, Zack!" Madison yelled, sounding truly frantic. The zombie moans were getting closer.

Zack yanked the Swiss Army knife from his pants pocket and pulled out the long blade. Sitting on the bed, he steadied the plastic bat on its end and jammed the metal point into the bottom, vigorously carving out a yellow parallelogram from the base. He picked up his oversize replica Coke bottle, piggy-banked with coins, and dumped it out in one huge pile next to the bat. Handful after handful, Zack funneled the change into the hollow plastic until it was brimming with ancient pennies caked in a diseased green fungus.

"Darn it!" Zack shouted, "I need tape."

Madison stuck a hand in her purse and riffled around. She plucked out a roll of duct tape and tossed it across the room.

"Came in handy once already," she quipped.

Zack taped off the bat's bottom and coiled more tape up the base for extra grip. He took a practice swing with the money-heavy bat.

Madison stepped back as Zack approached his grotesque sister. Now face-to-face with her kid brother, zombie Zoe strained ever harder, reaching tirelessly with both hands. Zack struck a batter's stance in front of the door.

"Zoe," he said, adjusting his grip and planting his feet firmly on the floor, "this is for . . . well, this is for everything, I guess." He wiggled his hips like a major leaguer at home plate.

"Wait!" Madison yelled, stepping in front of Zack. "Just don't break her nose, okay? She has such a cute little nose." She backed away, grimacing with anticipation.

Zack took a hard swing at Zoe's head and connected squarely with the dome of her zombie noggin. The cheap yellow plastic exploded in a sweet tinkling melody of silver and copper coins. Zack dropped the bat, and his monstrous sister slumped down, half in and half out of the room.

Madison patted Zoe's head as if to say, "good puppy" as she turned the doorknob and opened the door.

The zombie horde had reached the second-floor landing, spilling over one another, grappling mindlessly, clutching at nothing. Zack scooted past his sister and smiled at Madison.

"Was that fun for you or something?" she asked him.

"It was worth every penny," Zack said.

"You're such a dork."

The undead swarm clogged up the hallway, a tangled heap of shifting limbs, closing in slowly, steadily. Zack was nearly out of ideas, but he had one left.

"Madison," he said, "when Zoe sneaks out at night, how does she do it?"

"Easy. She climbs out her window and goes down the trellis."

Just then, one of the zombies tripped forward in a lurching half-stumble. Zack and Madison hopped back out of the way. The zombie hit the floor and crunched its face into the rug, which sounded a lot like squashing a beetle with the bottom of your shoe.

Zack grabbed Madison by the arm and hustled her down the hall. She shrugged off his grip, strutting away

from the zombie mob at her own leisurely pace. The soulless groans throbbed through the house, punctuated by high-pitched yaps and tiny paws scratching at the base of Zoe's bedroom door.

Zack pulled the door handle, and the puppy bolted out past Madison.

"Twinkles!" she shrieked as it went streaking between her legs. "No!"

CHAPTER

adison whirled around and watched in horror as her beloved pup barked ferociously at the zombies. But as the rowdy gang of scraggly beasts marched forward, the little dog's courage wilted in a pathetic whimper.

"Twinkles...come!" Madison ordered sternly. And as quick as he'd bolted out, Twinkles retreated back to Madison, who crouched down to scoop him up in her arms.

"Bad puppy!" she scolded him as Twinkles nuzzled and licked her face. Impatiently, Zack held the door for Madison and her nursling Boggle, an unfortunate crossbreed of a whining beagle and a bug-eyed Boston terrier.

The bedroom door clicked shut.

Zoe's room was a hot pink mess, all painted, draped, and covered with the girly color. The magenta walls were plastered floor-to-ceiling with glossy centerfolds of every heartthrob from Justin Timberlake to the Jonas Brothers. Zack gagged a little, sickened by the sight of his sister's tabloid shrine of chiseled faces.

He dashed to the window and peered out across the roof of the garage down at his mom's Volvo parked in the driveway. Madison followed Zack, sheltering the puppy bencath her arm.

"All right, Madison," Zack said, straining to pull up the window. "You and Twinkles first. We're gonna climb down the fence thingy and run for the car, okay?"

"You mean the *trellis*? The one with all the zombies climbing up?"

"Sure, trellis. Whatever.

Wait. What do you mean, 'climbing up'?"

Madison pointed to the side of the garage, where sure enough, four zombies were attempting to scramble their way to the top.

Luckily, the zombies weren't very coordinated, losing their balance mid-climb and falling to the ground repeatedly, hollow crunch after hollow crunch.

"Geez," said Zack. "Well, at least they can't get up here."

"They're already up here, genius." Just then, the room shook with a terrifying rattle as the upstairs zombies battered into the door. Twinkles growled and flashed his tiny teeth. Madison just stood there, petting the puppy's head.

"Are you not at all upset about the fact that we're about to die, Madison?" Zack paced back and forth, wading through piles of discarded Zoe outfits strewn across the floor.

"Of course, I'm upset," Madison said. "I missed the Evite to the End of the World party, and now I'm living out my precious last moments with you, you little freaka-zoid." Her words were filled with spite. "Where is Greg

Bansal-Jones when you need him?" She sighed wistfully.

If Madison was the prettiest girl in eighth grade, then Greg Bansal-Jones was the prettiest boy and definitely the meanest. Zack couldn't stand the lunkhead's stupid-sounding last name. And he would never forgive Greg for what he'd done to Rice in the bathroom. Greg and his two buddies had welcomed Rice back to school by flipping him upside down over the toilet bowl and dipping him headfirst into a triple chocolate fudge swirly. And sometimes, when the hallways of the school were quiet and empty, you could still hear Rice's screams echoing off the walls.

"Whatever, Madison, I'm trying, all right?" Zack said. "You and Greg and Zoe, you all think it's so cool to be mean. But if we don't get to that car down there in the next couple of minutes, you'll never have another chance to be a jerk to anybody ever again."

Madison withdrew into scornful silence in front of the window. Zack walked off into the connecting bathroom. The bedroom door rattled and creaked with the force of a dozen zombies.

Zack surveyed the windowless bathroom for another means of escape. Another weapon. *Come on, Zack,* he kept thinking. *There's always a way out.*

He flung open the towel closet and saw their only chance: the laundry chute. He couldn't believe he hadn't thought of it earlier. But there it was, and he knew where it led. Straight to the garage. Ground level. A quick hop-skip-jump to their sweet Volvo getaway.

"Madison, we're gonna be okay! We just have to go down the chute!"

"The laundry chute?" she asked from the other room. "You have got to be kidding."

"Hurry up! It's the only way out!"

"Zack, I'd rather be eaten alive than fall into a pile of your nasty underwear! Sick!"

Then came the sound of glass shattering and Madison's bloodcurdling shriek.

Zack rushed to the bathroom doorway and froze. The zombie crashed through the window, and Madison stumbled backward, tripping on the pink carpet. Zack recognized this zombie, too. It was Donnie Zimmer. Danny's twin brother.

Flat on his stomach, Donnie wiggled his hips, side to side, like a slug inching forward, panting, snorting, and grabbing at her heels. As he reached for Madison, his dingy yellowish skin stretched open, dripping blood down his arms, cut deeply from the sharp broken glass. Just before he lunged forward in a vicious, last-ditch bid to snatch her, Madison scrambled to her feet. Twinkles clung to her shirtsleeve, eyes boggling.

Madison brushed herself off and picked up her shoulder bag. The revolting corpse rose slowly from the floor and shuffled toward them. He wore a red, half-shredded T-shirt with a picture of a snake devouring its own tail.

"I thought you said these things can't climb," Madison said, catching her breath. Donnie Zimmer waddled across the room like some psychotic toddler.

"Yeah, well, at least they're super slow. . . ." Zack ushered Madison into the bathroom. The bedroom door started to crack, and the smothered zombie moan swelled through the fractured wood.

Zack gazed down into the dark, fathomless laundry chute and then back at Madison. "It's gonna be a tight squeeze." Madison shot him a sharp, devilish glare.

"What's that supposed to mean?" she asked.

"Nothing," Zack said. "You're bigger than me, that's all."

"Bigger?" she asked, steely-eyed. "I'm bigger than you? Why don't you just say what you *really* mean, Zachary?"

"What are you talking about, Madison?"

"That I'm too *fat* to fit down that disgusting chute . . ."

"Are you kidding me right now?" Zack

shouted with a growing sense of alarm. "We gotta go!"

The Zimmer zombie lurched nearer and nearer, and the ravenous horde of snaggletoothed hellhounds pulverized the bedroom door mercilessly. It was now little more than a gnarly blob of mutilated limbs and snapping jaws.

In spite of all this, Madison waited, arms crossed, chin raised, tapping her foot. Zack plucked up her bag and tossed it down the chute in a frenzy of impatience.

"Madison, come on!"

"I'm not going anywhere until you say something nice."

"Something nice," Zack blurted unwisely, holding out his hand for her to take.

"About me, you little runt," she said, playing kissy-face with Twinkles and scratching her pampered lapdog behind his ears.

Zack racked his brains for a quick, easy compliment, but with Madison that was not so easily done.

TAP
TAP

"You know what, Madison?" Zack paused.

The slavering ghouls tumbled into Zoe's bedroom, a hideous gush of belching mutants.

"If you want to stay here and get eaten, that's your problem."

And with that, he snatched Twinkles, climbed into the chute, and slid down, leaving Madison alone to decide her fate.

Zack rumbled down the old metal shaft, plummeting toward the garage. He held Twinkles snugly to his chest, and together they plunged into the stale stink of unwashed clothes.

Shaking off a pair of grass-stained jeans, he listened for Madison coming down after him, but he only heard the empty whoosh of the downdraft. Then, out of the buzzing hollow of the chute, a mind-ripping shriek echoed down to the garage. An eerie silence followed, and Zack felt a heart-sinking chill in the endless quiet.

"They got her . . . ?" Zack whispered in disbelief.

Twinkles cocked his head in confusion. "I guess it's just me and you now, Twinkie. . . ."

But before Zack could pick up the whimpering mutt from the laundry, the laundry chute thundered to life with a metallic clunk.

Zack and Twinkles watched as Madison flew headfirst into the musky hamper. She flung her arms and legs wildly, slinging off the Clarke family laundry every which way.

Madison stood up and turned to Zack. "I can't believe you left me up there with those Filthy McNasties," she said, punctuating every word with a fierce jab to

his scrawny chest.

But despite the dull pain of Madison's chest-poking onslaught, Zack couldn't stop the corners of his mouth from curling up into a grin.

"You think it's funny to leave a girl stranded like that?" she demanded.

Zack broke out in a fit of laughter, and it was then that Madison realized the joke was on her . . . literally.

In the midst of her tantrum, she'd neglected to notice the huge pair of tighty-whities hanging around her neck. She ripped them off her head quickly and threw them at Zack. *Puh-tooey!*

"Whose are those?" she squealed, repulsed.

"Must be Dad's," Zack giggled, stretching the elastic waistband a good two feet before flicking them away like a giant rubber band.

"Oh, that's sick." She shuddered, plucking Twinkles off the pile of laundry.

Zack pocketed his mother's car keys off a brass hook next to the switch for the garage door. Meanwhile, the zombies staggered just outside the garage. Madison peeked through the window, holding Twinkles. "Where did they all come from?" she asked, as Zack scanned the walls for a decent weapon.

"I don't know," he said, arming himself with a rusty ax.

"What do you think you're doing with that?" Madison asked him defiantly.

"You heard what Rice said." Zack swung the ax, and the edge whistled as it slashed through the air. "The only way to kill 'em is to chop off their heads."

"Zack, you can't just kill them," Madison argued. "They're people!"

"Wrong, Madison. They *used* to be people. Now they're dead people that don't know how to stay dead. It's a doggie dog world, Madison," Zack said. "I don't make the rules."

"No, *I* make the rules. And the rule is, no killing anything until we figure out what's going on out there," Madison said, stroking Twinkles's head. "And by the way, it's not doggie dog world, it's dog-*eat*-dog—"

WHAM! A rotting zombie arm smashed through the garage door right behind her. Madison jumped around, but the curdled, pulpy hand ripped Twinkles from her arms before she could step away.

Zack hopped over, ax raised, ready to hack through the grisly forearm, dangling severed veins off slabs of pruned flesh, but just before he brought down the blade, Twinkles sank his tiny fangs into the diseased

thumb. A small geyser of black juice squirted up from the puncture hole, and the pup squirmed free of the zombie death grip.

The gruesome arm drew back through the jagged hole in the garage door as Twinkles dropped to the cement. The ax head clanked on the floor with a bright orange spark. A torrent of pain shot up the wooden haft into Zack's wrists.

"Owww!" he yelped.

Madison rushed over to her puppy, and the frightened little dog scampered off hastily into the shadows.

"Twinkles?" she shouted. "Come back!" But Twinkles had already darted back into the house. Madison's big blue eyes narrowed with hate, her face a crazed scowl. She spun wildly around and stomped to the back of the garage. She came back from the junk-cluttered corner, wielding an old fire extinguisher.

"Open the door," she said in a tranquil daze, possessed now with the relaxed composure of divine vengeance.

"Are you sure that thing even works?" Zack asked skeptically.

Madison aimed the fire

extinguisher at Zack's feet and squeezed the pressure valve. The red tank hissed and gargled, and a fierce white spray shot from the black nozzle. "Now!" she commanded.

He dropped the ax and quickly pressed the button. The gears cranked overhead, slowly hoisting the garage door on its tracks. As the door lifted up, the overpowering stench of death seeped into the garage while the nitrous vapor seeped out.

Outside, the sluggish zombie brutes dragged their scuzzy feet toward the grinding screech of the rising door. Madison clutched the nozzle, her

thumb jittery on the shiny steel trigger.

The wretched dog-snatching zombie wobbled through the white foggy haze, and Madison shot a long blast of foam from the fire extinguisher. Blinded by the chemical froth, the zombie stumbled forward, flailing away at Madison.

She leaped to her right and dodged the foam-frosted ghoul, executing a textbook side kick that landed squarely in the zombie's lower back and sent the beast clanging into the garbage cans at the back of the garage.

"You like that, you walking pile of pus?" Madison shouted.

Pulling the car keys out of his pocket, Zack sprinted to the Volvo, unlocked the driver's side door, and hopped behind the wheel. He watched through the windshield as two more zombies shambled off the lawn toward the garage.

Madison aimed the extinguisher's nozzle at their rage-twisted faces, clicking the valve over and over, but the foam had run out. The zombies leaned as they hobbled, bones crooked in their sockets, faces curious and almost smiling as they limped toward Madison.

"Zack, do something!" Madison cried, backing across the blacktop.

Zack cranked the key in the ignition too far clockwise, causing a horrible chattering *screeeek,* and stretched his foot down to the pedal.

He slammed on the gas, and the Volvo lunged forward, colliding with the two bloodthirsty fiends. They soared off the bumper and sailed onto the lawn.

Zack slammed on the brakes and jumped out.

"Madison, you okay?" he asked.

Madison's stunned expression clicked back into focus as the Volvo began to roll slowly over the edge of the lawn.

She pushed Zack out of the way and hopped in the driver's seat. The tires stopped inches from the unconscious zombies splayed out over the front bushes. "You have to put it in park, moron," Madison said, returning to normal. She clicked on the head-lights. The zombies' wrinkling flesh gurgled in the harsh light.

Zack jumped in the passenger seat and buckled up. Madison swerved backward down the driveway, bounc-ing off the curb into the street. Zack stiffened against the seat back, eyes popping wide, as Madison slammed the accelerator and screeched off into the Phoenix night.

CHAPTER 7

Rice's house was dark and empty except for the bluish glow of the television flickering from the living room window. An abandoned backpack sat half-opened on the porch steps.

"That's his backpack," Zack whispered. "But I don't see Rice."

Madison puckered her lips in the rearview mirror. "How long are we supposed to wait for this kid?"

"I don't know. He should be right here." Zack put down the automatic window. "Psssst . . . Rice?" he called in a strained loud whisper.

"Oh, man, it reeks out there," Madison said, catching

a whiff of the rank, musty air wafting in from the humid night. She pinched her nostrils and breathed in through her mouth. "Eww, you can taste it, too."

Yeah, Zack thought. *This whole night stinks.* Just then, Rice stepped around the back corner of the house at the far end of the driveway. "Here he comes!" Zack exclaimed, pointing at the squat, husky silhouette waddling toward the street.

"Tell him to hurry up," Madison demanded.

"Rice, come on, man, we gotta get movin'!" Zack urged. But Rice didn't respond. He just kept lumbering slowly, swaying back and forth.

As he stepped out of the shadows, Rice's arms drifted in front of him, hanging as if by strings on a marionette. His face was spackled with blackened scabs and ripe pink pustules. "Raaaaghrr!" he groaned, approaching the street.

"That dude is *so* not getting in this car," Madison said, shifting out of park.

"Wait a second," Zack said, squinting at his friend.

Rice's eyes had the same blank stare as the others: that trancelike gaze that seemed to blur the difference between the living and the undead.

Suddenly, zombie Rice broke into a sprint and rushed the car. "Rraaaaarrghhh!!!" he growled, slapping the hood with a loud bang. Zack and Madison both screamed. "Brrrraaaiins!" Rice intoned. "Brraaaiiiiiins!" This was followed by a raspy chuckle.

Zack breathed a sigh of relief as his friend snapped back to humanity. Rice trotted over to the front porch, fetched his bag, and bounced into the backseat.

"I got you guys *good*," Rice gloated proudly before zipping up the backpack.

"Not funny, Rice," Zack said.

"Oh, lighten up, will you? I was only foolin' around."

Madison turned around and seized Rice by the shirt collar like an angry drill sergeant harassing a brazen rookie. But then, upon seeing his scabby face, she quickly released her grasp.

"Eeckhh," she grumbled. "What's up with all the zits?"

"It's not acne," Rice murmured. "It's chicken pox."

"Is he absolutely necessary?" Madison asked, turning to Zack.

"I'm afraid I am, *Madison*," Rice explained smugly. "For instance, I know that y*ou* need to know what I know. Because *I* know what we need to do. And right now what *we* need to do is to pick up ginkgo biloba."

"Is he the new exchange student from Tokyo?" Zack asked.

"It's not a 'he,' Zack. It's an 'it,'" Rice clarified. "And we're gonna need plenty of it if we plan on making it through the night."

"Ginkgo? That's your brilliant plan?" Madison

scoffed. "Have you even seen one of these things yet?"

"Zombies? Yeah, I've seen zombies," Rice said defensively. "I saw 'em all over the news. What's your point?"

"Well, Rice?" Madison spoke as if explaining something to a small child. "It's a little different when they're trying to rip your guts out." She steered the Volvo away from the curb into the empty street.

"No need to rub it in," Rice said, disappointed. "I'm jealous enough as is. My neighborhood's sooo boring." Rice lived in a tiny alcove of the city, all dead ends and one-ways. The zombie attack had missed the area completely.

"You actually want to see the zombies?" Madison was shaking her head. "Why?"

"For the same reason that people chase tornadoes. Because they're freakin' awesome!" Rice said. "But that's not the point. Based on my internet research, I've discovered that this ginkgo biloba stuff will, like, repel the zombies. Kind of like what garlic does to vampires. . . ."

"Kind of like what your pock-covered face does to me," Madison cracked.

"Is she always this funny, Zack?"

"I'm the funniest person you'll ever meet," Madison taunted, refusing to back down.

"Guys, relax," Zack intervened, raising his hands like a substitute teacher trying to regain control of a rowdy homeroom. "Did you hear anything important on the news, Rice?" Zack wanted facts, not one of Rice's half-baked theories.

"Well, I tried, but the reporter kind of got eaten in the middle of the broadcast."

"They ate him?" Madison said slowly, completely revolted.

"Yeah, totally. This one zombie came out of nowhere and was like 'Blaaahhh!' And then this other one chomped the guy's neck. And then blood spattered all over the camera lens, and then—"

"We got the picture, sicko," Madison said.

"Let's get back to the ginkgo," Zack prompted.

"Okay, now I don't know if it's the ginkgo or the biloba, but it's supposed to prevent cell damage, which zombies *do* have, improve blood flow, which zombies *don't* have, and increase brain function, which they *definitely* don't have. Plus, the ginkgo tree never gets diseases and it's completely insect resistant. It all ties together, man! Zombie garlic! Get it?"

Not really, Zack thought, staring like a zombie at his overzealous pal.

"That makes zero sense," Madison said.

"*You* make zero sense, *Madison,*" Rice jeered. "Zack, are you sure Zoe's the only person you clobbered over the head tonight? Should this girl even be driving? We're doing like five in a thirty."

"Shut up, creep!" Madison shouted, veering toward the curb. "I'm still getting the hang of it."

"Lay off, Rice. It's not like she has a license, and you can't even reach the pedals," Zack said.

"Sorry, Madison," Rice apologized reluctantly. "I didn't mean to dog you out like that."

"Dog . . . ?" Madison tapered off into a shrill whimper. Her eyes welled up with tears as she choked back the sobs. "Poor Twinkles!" The Volvo started to drift off-center again.

"Who's Twinkles?" Rice asked.

"Twinkles was . . . I mean, *is* her dog," Zack explained. "He got spooked and ran away."

"Oh, man. That sucks. You know they say that if zombies can't find human flesh to chow down on, they'll settle for smaller animals like squirrels or rodents or—"

"Dude!" Zack shouted.

"How do you even know this loser anyway?" Madison spluttered between sobs. "He's so mean!" The car veered across the middle of the road.

"He's my best friend," Zack admitted.

"This is your best friend, Zack?" Madison sniffled, regaining full control of the car. "You've got serious problems."

Just then, the Volvo bounced up and down as if it had hurtled too fast over a speed bump. Rice had neglected to buckle his seat belt and sprang up off the backseat.

Madison slammed the brakes. The car pitched to a halt in the middle of the road.

"Wh-what was that?" Zack stuttered.

The three of them flipped around, looking out the back window. All they could see was the empty road behind them.

"Should we get out and look?" Madison asked, preparing to unbuckle her seat belt.

Rice gasped as a bloated zombie woman rose off the pavement. She was stiff and twisted, wearing a torn shirt with a tire mark mudcaked across her stomach. Her dead silver eyes blazed red in the ruddy glow of the taillight. Purple drool oozed from her chapped, flaking mouth. The zombie woman pounced forward and latched on to the back of the car, snarling and shrieking.

"Go!" Zack yelled. Madison hit the gas. The rabid

ghoul clung to the back bumper.

"Aahhhhhh!" Madison cried, and jerked the steering wheel, which flung the zombie lady loose. She thumped and rolled onto the grassy lawn.

"Watch out, Madison," Zack warned as they swerved from side to side. "They're everywhere!"

The road ahead was filled with freshly risen corpses, awakening like dominoes in reverse. The Volvo zigzagged gradually through the zombie obstacle course, but there was a much more serious problem ahead. A dense pack of the walking dead was making its way across the street, like a zombie parade, right where they needed to turn.

"Madison, step on it!" Rice shouted.

"But we're gonna crash into them," she pleaded.

"Just go!" yelled Zack.

Madison dipped around the final zombie and mashed the accelerator. The engine bellowed. The needle metered. Twenty mph! Thirty!

"Faster," Zack hollered. Forty mph!

The zombies blundered through the crosswalk.

A putrid, nauseating procession of the damned, narrowing the gap to the corner.

They all held their breath, and just before the throng of mutants reached the sidewalk, Madison spun the steering wheel to the right.

The tires screeched, jumping the curb, and Zack, Rice, and Madison shifted to the left of the skidding car, stunned into silence. The front bumper barreled through a blue mailbox on the corner, sending up a flurry of white envelopes and glossy catalogs. And now the Volvo was careening straight into a telephone pole.

CHAPTER 8

Madison swerved, dodging the crash. She straightened the wheel as hard as she could, and the tires regained their grip on the black-top with an earsplitting screech. When the smoke cleared from the burnt rubber, the parade of zombies was behind them.

"We made it!" Zack shouted.

"That was insane!" said Rice.

Madison pressed the brakes, and the car sputtered to a halt. Zack stared through the windshield at the crumpled hood of the Volvo. *How am I going to explain that one?* he thought, rubbing the headache from his temples.

"Before we go any farther," Madison announced, "I just have to say that I'm totally uncomfortable shopping anywhere but Whole Foods."

"We're not shopping," Rice corrected. "We're gathering the zombie garlic, remember?"

"Whatever, maggot," Madison conceded. "Where is this place?"

"Two more blocks," Rice said.

"All I'm saying," she continued, "is that Whole Foods has a much healthier selection than this Albertsons place."

The Volvo coasted down the block, snaking down the double yellow lines. Up ahead, a Channel 7 news van idled on the side of the road. The satellite dish fastened to the top rotated briefly and flashed red. Rolling by, they noticed the sliding side door left open. Behind the wheel, the driver was stuffing his mouth with a greasy double-chili cheeseburger.

"Gross!" Madison sneered.

The burger-gobbling van driver swallowed his last gulp of the slimy fast food, slowly hinging and unhinging his jaw. Suddenly, the man's spine went straight and rigid. He began shaking rapidly. The bits of soggy bun flew from his mouth in a deep, barking cough. He convulsed hard with three quick spasms, slumped over in the seat, and went limp.

"Yo, did you see that?" Rice asked. "Did he just choke to death?"

"We should go see if he's okay," Madison said, hitting the brakes.

"No way," Rice answered quickly. "Every man for himself."

They turned around and looked through the rear

windshield. A fat, bearded guy was lugging a giant news camera. A hysterical woman with red hair trotted behind him in high heels, carrying a microphone. They were racing back to the van.

"What are they running from?" Zack said.

"Whaddaya think, idiot?" Madison replied.

Just as the Channel 7 duo reached the news van, the unconscious driver pounced out of the front seat and mauled the cameraman like a rabid cougar.

"Duuude! Can we get out of here, please?" Rice yelled.

But straight ahead, more zombies wandered down the main drag and into the supermarket parking lot.

The asphalt shimmered with a thousand shards of glass. Garbage wrappers swirled in a hot gust of wind around the zombies' shuffling feet.

Albertsons was completely infested. The groping herd thrashed down the well-stocked aisles, wreaking havoc inside the store.

"I told you we should have gone to Whole Foods," Madison said.

"We're not going to Whole Foods, all right? It's

twenty minutes away. Turn around. There's another Albertsons, like, six blocks from here," Rice commanded.

Suddenly, something slapped against the windshield.

"Ahhh!" Madison yelled.

But it was just a grease-soaked fast-food wrapper. A cartoon logo of a smiling dachshund with a head shaped like a hamburger, its long body like a hot dog, smiled back at them.

"Ick!" Madison shrieked and turned on the windshield wipers.

"What the heck is BurgerDog?" Zack asked Rice, reading the wrapper through the windshield.

"You haven't seen the commercials? It's this new fast-food joint. They're opening up all over the country this weekend. It's a hot dog that looks like a hamburger. Or something like that. . . ."

"Nasty." Madison hit the gas.

The second Albertsons loomed in the distance, taking up almost half a block on the main street. Madison pulled into the empty lot and parked the Volvo. The trio hopped out and stalked up under the blue awning that hung over the front of the deserted store. They peered inside through the long line of large glass windowpanes. Rice yanked the handle of the automatic door, but it wouldn't budge. He pushed the blue handicapped button over and over, but nothing happened.

"Okay, Ginkgo Boy," Madison said, "How are we supposed to get inside?"

"Follow me." Rice waved them along. Creeping down the alley past the loading docks, he led the way around back.

The rear of the grocery store was a flat two-story slab of cement. On both sides, fire escapes slashed down from red doors at the top corners of the building. At ground level, two big black double doors flanked an industrial-size blue Dumpster in the center of the outside wall. Above the Dumpster there was a half-open window.

Rice pried with his fingernails at the back service entrances, but both were barred and locked from the inside.

"Brilliant, Rice," Madison said. "Where would we be without you?"

"Whole Foods?" he quipped.

"There!" Zack scaled up the blue steel edge of the garbage-filled Dumpster. Steadying himself, he slid the window all the way up, then squiggled through the opening. He dropped into the dark storage room.

Madison climbed up next, squeamish at the pit of reeking trash. Then came Rice, wheezing. He clung to Madison's shoulder to catch his balance.

"Hands off, dork!" she sneered.

"Your wish is my command," Rice said, scratching around a swollen chicken pock bubbling up on his cheek.

"Eww . . ." Madison muttered under her breath.

"Itchy," Rice explained.

Inside, Zack found a small stepladder to stand on and reached his hand through the window. Madison quickly volunteered. She knelt awkwardly on the ledge and ducked her head, pausing halfway through.

"What's the matter now?" Zack said.

"My shirt's caught," Madison said.

"Oh, come *on,*" Rice said.

"No! This is Juicy Couture," she said, carefully pulling at the fabric. "There, got it!" She lost her balance suddenly, and her back foot kicked off the windowsill, slamming Rice in the neck, and sending him belly flopping into the heap of ripe, slimy garbage.

"Aahhhhhh!" he screamed.

Madison toppled forward onto Zack, who smacked the back of his skull with a dull thud on the hard linoleum floor. A woozy rush flooded his head. His vision speckled, and the room faded to black.

"Zack! Zack!" Madison shouted, jostling his shoulders.

Three blurry Madisons hovered above him. The two fuzzier Madisons on the right and left merged back into the real Madison in the middle. Their eyes met and flicked away.

"What? What's going on?" he asked.

"I'm sorry, Zack. That was totally my fault," Madison admitted.

Behind them, Rice clambered up through the window, groaning painfully. He was stuck, his pudgy gut seesawing on the window's ledge. A black-spotted banana peel slid off his head. "Help," he grunted. Madison strolled over, rolling her eyes.

"But you're covered in trash. . . ." She hesitated, brushing him off slightly.

"Please, Madison!"

"Fine," she said.

Madison's hands squished into Rice's soggy, garbage-soaked sweatshirt as he wormed his way over the ledge. "This is too disgusting," she said, letting him fall.

Rice crashed face-first onto the floor. He curled up like a large potato bug, wincing in agony.

Zack sat dazed in a sullen lump, rubbing his head. Madison tromped over and wiped off her grimy Rice-hands on Zack's sleeves. Straightening his glasses, Rice rummaged around in his backpack and pulled out two flashlights. He waggled the bright, shining light on Zack's unresponsive face.

"Stop that!" Zack squinted angrily and blocked the blinding beam with his palm. "Let's just go gather up the 'bingo globula' and see if you're right."

"Ginkgo biloba," Rice corrected. "And it's gonna work."

"More like geeko blobola," Madison joked. "And it better work."

CHAPTER 9

Moonlight shimmered in through the glass storefront, sparkling off the polished floor. Standing by the long row of conveyor-belted registers, Zack, Madison, and Rice stared outside into the immense parking lot.

"They can smash right through there," Zack said.

"Easily," Madison said.

"Bet that's awesome," Rice muttered, fetching a shopping cart from behind the checkout lanes.

They crept up and down the towering aisles and tiptoed into the vitamin section, stocked with big white tubs of protein powders and dark brown plastic containers labeled with all the letters of the alphabet. *Zinc. No. Calcium. Nope. Garlique . . . Cod liver oil. Echinacea? St. John's wort? What is all this junk?* Zack thought.

"Ginkgo biloba! Here it is!" Zack said.

They swept clean the four rows of anti-zombie tablets into the shopping cart. As they rolled their stash to the back of the store, Zack watched Madison's horrified reflection in the rounded glass of the butcher case. Raw chicken carcasses were on display, along with dead-eyed fish and jumbo shrimp, not to mention the slabs of flank steak and mounds of ground beef. They stopped in the dim blue perma-glow of the frozen-food section, where they spotted an elevator. They carted the ginkgo onto the lift and rose to the second floor.

Upstairs, the doors shut behind them, and Rice, Madison, and Zack gazed down the long corridor. A pale blue wedge of light shone through the thin slit of a door, slightly ajar, at the end of the hall. A placard on the door read MANAGER'S OFFICE.

The shopping cart wheels squeaked as they pushed

through the open door. Inside, the floor was a wide expanse of dirty beige tiles, and the ceilings were too low. In the near corner, a cheap tasseled throw rug covered the floor in front of a brown vinyl sofa, which sat opposite a big flat-screen television. Farther down the same wall, a doorway led to a small kitchen equipped with a sink, a fridge, and a couple of dirty counters. A cockroach skittered behind the microwave. The whole office was painted puke green, and it stank of sour mop water.

"This place is perfect," Rice said, spinning around.

"You have got to be kidding," Madison muttered.

Zack steered the shopping cart over to the desk and unloaded the ginkgo biloba. He dumped out a mountain of gray capsules on the manager's desk and snapped one in half. A small dose of powder spilled on the desk calendar. "How much of this stuff do we need?" Zack asked.

"A whole lot, man," Rice said, looking at his reflection in a mirror. He was inspecting the red spots covering his face. "Madison, you better help him out," Rice said as he pulled a small prescription bottle of pink liquid and a few Q-tips from his sweatshirt pocket. He twisted off the cap and daubed at his pox with the pink, goopy cotton swab.

"This was your idea, you nasty little pock mongrel," Madison complained.

Rice plopped down on the sofa and kicked up his feet. His face was dappled with soothing pink splotches. "Chicken pox is no joke, man. Not too long ago people died from the pox."

"I better open a window." Madison shot Rice a meaningful glance. "There's a lot of hot air blowing in here." She slid open the big window looking over the parking lot and joined Zack at the desk.

By now Zack had cracked open nearly a dozen capsules, and the small pile of ginkgo was still barely an anthill.

Rice sighed and found the remote control wedged in the seat cushion. He flipped on the television.

"This live news report is brought to you by . . . BurgerDog. *The burger that tastes like a dog!*" the commercial voice announced. Then the smirking animated wiener dog waddled on-screen and barked. Its head was shaped like a burger with its ears sprouting out of the bun, and its nose grew out of the flesh-colored meat patty.

"Are you gonna help us or what, Rice?" Zack hollered.

The television returned to the eleven o'clock news with breaking reports on the zombie infestation: "Welcome back, Phoenix. This is Cliff Hemmings keeping you updated on what is turning out to be, quite literally, the *Night of the Living Dead*. And apparently we are not alone. This is happening all over the country!"

"Did you hear that?" Rice asked. "This is going on all over the place!"

"Rice, this is taking forever," Zack complained, tapping out the contents of another pill.

Madison began to hammer the ginkgo capsules with the heel of her shoe. She kept slamming until the white ginkgo powder puffed up into the air.

"Stop!" Rice shouted. "Are you crazy?"

"What's the problem?" she said happily, displaying

the fresh mound of ginkgo dust, like a perky game show assistant.

"Don't you know that zombies have long-range hearing?" Rice scolded.

"Well, saw-ree," Madison said, slipping her foot back into her sneaker.

The news broadcast cut to a red-haired reporter with a microphone.

"Hey." Zack pointed. "It's that news lady from the street." Madison and Rice quit bickering and looked.

The red-haired reporter spoke in a frenzied, fast-paced voice: "Here we are at the grand opening of the new fast-food chain BurgerDog. What began as a fun, family, free-burger giveaway has since turned into a wild melee of eat or be eaten. These zombies you are watching appeared out of nowhere. . . ." As she spoke, a teenage boy wearing a soccer uniform bounded out of the zombie mayhem in the background and raced up behind the newswoman, bobbing and weaving. He gave a head-fake in front of the camera and dashed out of the frame.

"Was that just . . . ?" Zack couldn't believe it.

"Greg Bansal-Jones!" Madison gushed.

Mooowahhhhhaaargghhhhh!

"Did you guys just hear that?" Rice flipped off the television.

"Rice, quit messing around," Zack said.

"It wasn't me, dude. . . ."

Mooooowaaaaahhhhhhhaaargh!

CHAPTER 9

Zack, Rice, and Madison listened to the hammering of their pulses. Seconds ticked off like slow minutes as they waited, transfixed, in the awful silence that followed the hollow zombie howl.

Moooowaaaaaahhhaaarrgh! It was the unmistakable zombie battle cry.

"Where is it coming from?" Zack asked. He ran to the door of the office and looked out into the hallway. Nothing.

Moooowaaaaaahhhaaarrgh!

Bang! Crack! Pop! The windows rattled and snapped, and the wind-chime jingle of falling glass drowned out the rabid moans.

"They're out front!" Madison cried, racing to the window. The boys followed.

The zombie horde crowded under the blue awning, filing in through the shattered storefront.

"Quick! We have to try and go around how we came in!" Zack said.

They ran out of the office, down the hall, pausing at the slow elevator, and then raced down the cement stairwell instead.

Down the shadowy aisles of the grocery store, a pack of thirty zombies, maybe more, throttled through the tabloids. A grizzly hand pounded one of the cash registers open. Zombie pus-blood drizzled on the neat stacks of greenbacks.

The trio dashed to the back of the store and plowed through the plastic curtain strips under a sign over the doorway marked EMPLOYEES ONLY. They jogged down the dark corridor lit up at the end by a glowing red EXIT sign. Zack lifted the metal bar off the back of the door. Madison and the boys peered outside.

The back lot was crammed with zombies, like a

mosh pit at a heavy metal concert. A hundred sickly eyes gazed at them crazily. No way out.

Zack slammed the door, and they heard a dull, bony crunch. The door bounced back open with a zombirific howl. A knotted, big-knuckled hand was slotted in the gap by the hinges, four fingers now fractured at the base, still wriggling. Zack and Madison pushed on the black door, as the mad-staggering flock moved toward the back entrance. Rice took several steps backward and then hurled himself, ramming his full weight into the doorjamb. *BAM!* They were safe. And the zombie hand was gone. Sort of.

Rice's body slam had severed the zombie's fingers, and now they were jumping around on the floor. Zack placed the bar back on the door. Madison's mouth gaped with disgust.

"Awesome!" Rice pulled his fist down, elbow to hip. "Now we have specimens."

"What do you mean . . . specimens?" Madison asked.

"I saw this one movie where zombies took over

the entire world, and these scientists needed specimens for testing at the lab." Rice produced a Ziploc bag from his backpack and gathered the squirmy fingers off the ground. He swung the see-through bag in front of Madison's face.

"Zack, make him stop!" Madison squealed. But Zack was already running back into the store.

"Zack!" they screamed. "Where are you going?"

By the time Madison and Rice caught up to him, he was dodging zombies and dragging heavy bags of charcoal briquettes over to the elevator.

"We're gonna have a barbecue," he explained. Rice and Madison stared at him blankly. "Just help me load these up."

The zombies were closing in fast, already halfway up the food aisles.

"Rice. You have to unload those bags and bring them to the office. Okay?"

"All by myself?"

"I'll help him," Madison volunteered, hopping on the elevator.

"I'll get the lighter fluid," Zack said. "Send down the elevator when you're done. I'll meet you up top. . . ." The elevator doors shut.

Zack darted down Household Goods aisle 7 and ripped open a box of black trash bags, tossing in a long box of matches. He swept a row of lighter fluid off the top shelf and into the garbage bag.

But Zack was not the only one shopping.

A deranged zombie couple thrashed at the shelves, knocking off an array of paper towels and aerosol spray cans.

The zombie woman looked like she hadn't slept in a year. Dark bags of flesh sagged under her bloodshot eyes. Her left ear was missing, and streaks of blood poured down her neck. She wore a T-shirt that read I'M WITH STUPID →.

Stupid didn't look any better. Both his lips were gone, leaving a jagged bloodstained gash where the bottom half of his face should have been. His gums had shriveled, exposing the roots of his teeth. It looked like he had just won first place in a cherry pie–eating contest.

Mr. and Mrs. Zombie advanced, wrenching forward in abrupt robotic bursts.

Zack skidded around the corner with his plastic satchel of flammable loot, but more zombies were now blocking his route to the stairwell. With no other choice, Zack scaled the shelves to the top.

The supermarket was jam-packed, zombies everywhere. They lumbered in all directions, displaying every symptom of meat-craving insanity.

A dozen zombie arms stretched up out of their sockets and grabbed at Zack's feet. He stomped at the groping

hands and then took a flying leap over the drooling beasts below.

He landed slightly off balance, and the unsteady shelving unit teetered and swayed, threatening to tip. One false move and the thing was going to collapse. He clasped his hand around the top of the garbage bag and prepared to jump.

Just then, the whole unit tipped backward, setting off a domino effect of toppling shelves that buried the zombies in a heap of bent metal, chunky salsa, cheese curls, and two-liters.

Zack trampled down the crunching pile of junk food and zombie claws and then hid in a clearing behind a bargain bin of assorted DVDs: *Happy Feet, Surf's Up, Don't Look Now.*

Zack gasped, eyeing the door to the stairwell.

A tank-topped, hairy-shouldered zombie with a curly mullet stood barefoot in front of the door, wearing boxer shorts dotted with smiley faces. He squished his eyeball against the thin, crosshatched window.

Above the elevator the number two was still lit up.

C'mon, Rice, send it back down already, Zack thought, clutching the bag. He glanced over his right shoulder.

A pretzel-legged zombie cheerleader pulled herself across the smooth linoleum with the sticky palms of her hands. *Slap, slap . . . pull. Slap, slap . . . pull.* Her legs were useless, dislocated at the hips, and a scaly red scab masked half of her face. She looked at Zack with a demented stare.

The zombie blocking the stairwell whipped its head around too fast. Its right eye sprang from the deep purple socket hole like a rubber ball off a wooden paddle. It made a sound like when you pop the inside of your cheek with your index finger. Murky orange saliva poured down the chin of the jut-jawed slob.

Ding!

Finally the number one lit up. The doors opened, and Zack made a break for the elevator.

He was seriously off balance, sprinting faster than his feet could carry him, and he caught a glimpse of the eyeball swaying by a blue stretchy tendon.

The squelching ghoul shuffled across the tiles.

Its swollen feet slogged across the floor, leaving a slippery trail of gray-green goop. Zack hit the floor, sliding chest-first, and skidded between the juicy beast's legs, which were covered in a cruddy pus. The zombie bent suddenly at the waist, and his flabby arms swiped down. The dangling eyeball swung like a pendulum and whacked Zack behind his ear. *Aahhh, nasty!* Zack glided into the elevator, arms outstretched like a slip-n'-slime Superman. The bag of lighter fluid clanked on the closing doors, and the elevator car lifted.

His whole front now stained with zombie muck, Zack burst through the office door and dumped out the black trash bag next to the three bags of charcoal. He ripped open the tops of the charcoal bags and squeezed the first bottle of lighter fluid, dousing the sooty black rocks.

Suddenly, Zack realized he was alone in the room. He whirled around twice before noticing two heads bobbling outside the open window behind the desk.

Perched on the awning above the crowd of zombies, Rice and Madison crawled on their hands and knees. Rice had snipped two holes in the awning with a pair of scissors from the manager's desk, and they were each armed with a squirt gun from Rice's backpack. They aimed their plastic pistols down through the holes and watered the beastly wrangle below them.

"Rice, what are you doing?" Zack shouted through the window.

"Watch and learn, Zack," Rice said, blasting a zombie with a long stream from the squirt gun. "We dissolved the ginkgo in the water guns and now . . ."

"This isn't working, Rice!" Madison yelled over the savage groans.

"Keep squirting!" he commanded like a little general.

"Will you two stop squirting zombies and help me in here? I have a real idea."

"Not now, Zack!"

"Fine, I'll do it myself." Zack squeezed out another bottle of lighter fluid on the open bags of charcoal and carried one over to the window. Rice and Madison crawled back inside the office.

"I told you it wouldn't do anything," Madison said. "It just ticked them off."

"It would've worked if you squirted them in the mouth," Rice said. "She's got horrible aim, Zack."

"Who came up with this ginkgo theory of yours anyway?"

"I did," Rice said proudly.

I knew it, Zack thought, shaking his head while lugging the charcoal.

"Okay, so . . . who made you the zombie science expert?" asked Madison.

"I had a hunch," Rice explained. "You know the feeling when genius strikes, and you just know something?"

Madison furrowed her eyebrows and blinked three times in a row. "Does anybody have a better idea?" *Blink. Blink. Blink.*

"I do!" Zack shouted, dropping the bag on the floor, "You guys bring over the rest of the charcoal and pass me the bags through the window."

"What for?" Rice asked.

"Just do it!" Zack ordered, and crawled onto the awning.

Obediently, Rice and Madison carried over the remaining two bags to Zack.

He edged cautiously around the border of the canopy and poured out the wet black charcoal, forming a boundary around the snarling horde underneath the awning.

Zack looked out at the Volvo parked well past the zombie danger zone.

"Now bring me the matches. But come out real slow, I don't know how long this thing's gonna hold us."

Madison climbed out first. Rice followed with his ginkgo-filled survival pack strapped to his back. Madison handed Zack the box of matches.

He sparked a match and dropped it gently off the side. The tiny flame disappeared as the match head sputtered onto the charcoal border. A zombie hand tore a hole up through the awning. Its slimy finger grazed Madison's ankle.

"We're all going to die!" she shouted.

Just then a fearsome blaze shot up around the wailing zombies, barricading them underneath the awning. Tall flames spewed up from the hedge of fire, scorching the canopy.

All three of them peered over the smoking edge.

"One . . ." Rice counted.

"Two . . ." Madison said next.

The canvas started to rip under their feet. The underside of the blue fabric sizzled open with brown burn holes,

revealing the shrieking monsters beneath them.

"Three!" Zack yelled, and they jumped as far away from the fiery awning as their legs could thrust them— which wasn't very far.

They hit the ground running and raced for the parking lot.

Two blazing ghouls staggered through the flames and onto the walkway. Rice tripped on a long yellow speed bump and fell flat on his stomach. He squirmed desperately under the weight of his backpack, like a fish flopping on the beach.

"Help!" Rice cried. Madison skidded to a halt.

The scorched zombies lurched over Rice's wriggling figure. Their melting skin dripped on the asphalt like hot wax.

Madison broke into a sprint.

CHAPTER

She hoisted Rice to his feet by his shoulder strap, just in time, and they took off running.

"You just saved my life, Madison," Rice huffed.

"I know. I should have my head examined."

Safely inside the car now, Madison sped out of the parking lot in a burst of hysterical rubber. Zack stuck his head out the window and sighed. He sniffed the night air, still ripe with the musky tang of meat gone bad.

"Zack, put up the window, man." Rice coughed. "You shouldn't be breathing that stuff."

"We've been breathing the air all night and nothing's happened, Rice," Zack said, slumping back down in his seat. "Stop being so paranoid."

"Please roll up the window, Zack. That smell is awful," Madison said calmly, focused behind the wheel.

Zack buzzed up the window, and Madison nodded thank-you. Rice rolled his eyes, and Zack flicked on the radio.

A long, high-pitched beep pierced their eardrums. Zack clasped both sides of his head. The beeping stopped, and an electronic voice recording came over the speakers, half human, half machine: "This is not a test. Repeat. This is not a test. The Emergency Alert System has been activated by the president to inform all United States citizens of the grave national crisis unfolding. All survivors in the Phoenix area should proceed directly southbound to the Tucson Air Force Base."

"Tucson . . . ? Tucson, Tucson?" Zack stammered.

"That's like over an hour from here, guys," Madison whined. "And I've never driven on the highway before."

"We have no other choice," Zack said.

The voice came back on the radio: "All drivers are advised to stay inside of their vehicles until they reach

their designated military outpost. The source of the infection is still unknown. . . . *Beeeeeeeeep* . . ."

"Whoa, whoa, whoa," Madison said, slowing down at a stop sign.

Just ahead of them, the block teemed with hundreds of zombies. They drifted drowsily, like crazed sleepwalkers.

"Sick. . . ." Madison shuddered.

"Sick!" Rice smiled.

A teenage zombie wearing a BurgerDog polo shirt and server's cap turned to face them. His left knee buckled backward, and he tottered with an excruciating sidelong limp. His head tilted to the right where the

side of his neck was missing a large hunk. The drive-through headset and microphone were still clamped to his head. Zack did not want fries with that.

Madison made a wide left turn away from the zombie-laden street.

"Didn't that guy in the news van choke to death on a burger and then attack that camera guy?" she asked.

"Do you think the burger had something to do with it?" Zack asked.

"I think it's a little weird, that's all," Madison said. "One minute he's eating a burger and the next minute he's turning into a zombie."

"Not possible. Hamburgers don't turn people into

zombies, Madison," Rice said defiantly. "Besides, you have to be bitten by a zombie to become one of them—"

"Wait, Madison, where are you going? We need to get on the highway," Zack said, realizing that they were headed straight back into his neighborhood.

"And we will," she replied. "But first we have to go back to your house and find Twinkles. He's probably scared half to death. Plus, I forgot my bag."

"But that's Zombie Central back there!" Rice hollered from the backseat.

"I don't care. I'm not abandoning my dog, you little rodent," Madison yelled.

"You heard the radio," Rice protested, "I'm pretty sure it said don't get out of your car and start searching for lost mutts."

"Twinkles is not a mutt. He's a Boggle mix," Madison shot back.

"You named your boy dog Twinkles?" Rice asked.

"I'm sorry, isn't your name *Rice*?"

"Actually, it's Johnston. *Last* name's Rice. And I don't care that your dog's a mutt or that you gave it a stupid name," Rice said. "All I care about is getting out of town. Not driving back into it! Zack, can you back me up, please?"

"I—I don't know, Rice. . . ." Zack hesitated. "Maybe if Madison goes back for Twinkles, then we could maybe find Zoe and you know . . . help her."

"Have you lost your mind? Your sister's a goner, dude. There's no cure for zombies," Rice tried desperately to explain.

"Oh yeah, and what if there is?" Madison retorted.

"Rice, my parents would kill me if they found out I left Zoe behind," Zack argued.

"Our parents might even be zombies right now. We could be orphans for all you know!" A grim silence followed Rice's dreadful notion.

"We might be the last people on earth when this whole thing's over," Madison thought aloud.

"Just the three of us," Zack affirmed.

"We'll be responsible for repopulating the planet," Rice smirked.

"Don't get any ideas, Freako Suave," Madison said. And just like that, they drove off: two against one. Three against the world.

CHAPTER 12

The Volvo made a right onto Locust Lane, and they moved slowly down the road toward Zack's house. The blacktop was stained with crimson streaks, shining in the glitter of the streetlamps. The green lawns were drizzled in trails of cherry red. White picket fences were dashed with blood. Tipped-over trash cans lay sideways on the sidewalk and in driveways, spilling garbage all over.

"Where'd they all go?" Zack asked.

"To find us, probably," Madison said.

"Rice, I don't get it, man," Zack started. "You're saying the only way to turn into a zombie is if one of them bites you. So who bit the first zombie?"

"Chicken and the egg." Rice flipped his hand in the air. "There are tons of theories, guys: Meltdown at a cryogenics lab. Toxic biochemical waste. Nuclear radiation. Extraterrestrial radiation. Aliens taking over our brains—now that's what we should *really* be worrying about. . . ."

"He doesn't actually believe in aliens, does he?" she asked, steering steadily down the road. Zack nodded silently.

"Madison, if I told you yesterday to expect an all-out zombie invasion tomorrow, what would you have done?"

"I would have made fun of you for being a *loser*." Madison slowed in front of Zack's demolished house. "Then again, I probably would have done that anyway."

"Fine, but if there are zombies, that means there could be vampires. There could be werewolves. Bigfoot could really exist. Even Pigman. And Mothman. The Loch Ness monster. The Yeti. El Chupacabra—"

"Stop talking, dork. We're supposed to be on the lookout for Twinkles," Madison barked.

"And Zoe, too," Zack added, scoping out how badly his lawn had been trashed.

"Yeah," Rice scoffed. "I'm sure she'll be tough to miss."

They rolled into the driveway. Nearing the garage, Zack surveyed the damage through the windshield.

"Yo, Zack, they totally wrecked your house!" Rice exclaimed.

Rice was right. Zack's home was demolished. The lawn was trampled into bloody mud puddles, and the front garden was in shambles. The door was ripped off its hinges, the entrance reduced to rubble.

Every last window had been shattered.

"Why would aliens want to take over our brains in the first place?" Madison asked, unbuckling her seat belt.

"For the same reason zombies want to eat our brains," Rice said, sort of twist-hopping off the back-seat.

"Which is what?" Madison asked snottily, leading the way toward the front of the house.

"To gain our knowledge," Rice answered. "Which is probably why they haven't bothered with you all that much."

"Hey, buddy," Madison said defensively, "there are tons of zombies out there just dying to eat my brains."

"Look at this," Zack said, interrupting their quarrel. He picked up a bit of paper stuck in the bush off the front stoop. "It's another one of those wrappers."

"BurgerDog," Madison jeered. "That just sounds so gross."

"The hot dog that looks like a hamburger," said Rice, bungling the slogan.

"Maybe this *is* what the news van guy was eating,"

Zack proposed.

"Duh . . ." Madison sneered.

"It could have been anything, you guys. Wendy's, McDonald's, Burger King, you name it . . ." Rice said, disregarding Madison's theory.

"But what if it wasn't anything, Rice? What if it was this thing? What if Madison's right?" Zack asked.

Rice threw his hands up in frustration.

"Shut up," Madison shushed. "I'm going inside. . . ." She stepped cautiously into the house through the mangled archway of rutted wood and shattered glass that now comprised the entrance. "Twinkles?"

She nearly lost her footing on the slick layer of zombie slime coating the hardwood. Rice and Zack followed closely behind. Crossing the threshold, they squish-squashed through the residue of slippery sludge.

Suddenly, they heard a tiny bark coming from the living room.

"Twinkles!" Madison said excitedly, running into the room. She skated into the doorway and let out an ear-piercing scream. "NO!"

Zack and Rice hurried over, sliding in behind her. Rice hit a slick spot and fell with a splat, gliding into the wall.

Zombie Zoe whipped her beastly head around and roared at Zack and Madison. Clenching the poor little Boggle in her right hand, Zoe beat her chest, puppy-fisted, like King Kong at the top of the Empire State Building.

"Zoe," Madison squeaked, address-ing her monstrous BFF. "I don't care that you're already dead, or that you can't understand what I'm saying . . . but if you don't put my dog down, I'm going to kill you!"

"That's not very vegan of you, Madison," Rice said, rising from his puddle of muck, a bloody black skid mark skunk-striping his back.

Zack hurried around the couch and picked up a vase from the mantel. Swooping in behind his zombified sister, he raised the vase and smashed her on the head, resulting in a blast of jagged porcelain fragments.

Zoe reeled forward, her head slumping to her chest as she dropped to her knees. She wobbled for a second before tipping flat on her face, knocked unconscious.

Twinkles splashed across the floor, pawing through the living room mire. He scampered over to Madison, who lifted the little dog high in the air and twirled him around and around joyously.

Zack stood over his mutant sister, who hog-grunted into the wet hardwood. Madison sloshed over to Zack, cuddling Twinkles.

"Zack, that was so brave!" Madison exclaimed gratefully. "I'll never forget how you saved Twinkles's life. Ever." She brushed her hair to one side and leaned toward

Zack, giving him a kiss on his cheek. "And Twinkles won't either, will you, Twinkles?"

Zack's face reddened, and he wiped off the glossy mark that Madison's lips left on the side of his face. "It was nothing," he gushed goofily. He suddenly wished there were more puppies around that needed rescuing.

"All right, kids," Rice said. "You got your little pooch and you got your little smooch—now it's time to saddle up and hit the road."

"Rice, I can't just leave Zoe behind chewing people up and spitting them out."

"But she's doing what she loves," Rice replied. "You don't want to take that away from her, do you?"

"Sorry, Rice. I know she's a zombie, but she's also my sister."

"Fine, but if we're bringing her along, we're gonna do it my way." Rice disappeared and returned promptly, carrying a lacrosse helmet, a leash, and a dog collar that had once belonged to Zack's beloved pet boxer, Mr. BowWow.

"What're you doing with that?" Zack asked. "That's Mr. BowWow's."

"Well, since you insist on bringing your zombie sister along for the ride, we're gonna have to take some precautions. The helmet will protect us from her bites if she wakes up. . . . Help me out, will you?" Rice said, crouching down next to Zoe's limp body. "Now lift her head up so I can put it on."

Zack lifted the deadweight of his sister's skull while Rice fitted the lacrosse helmet over Zoe's tangled, matted hair. "There," Rice said, dropping her with a clunk as he fashioned her neck with the dog collar and leash. "Gotcha!"

Outside, Madison retrieved her bag from the garage and slurped her pink water.

Zack dragged Zoe through the front of the house by the leash.

"Are you sure it's okay dragging her like this?" Zack asked, pulling Zoe over the heap of debris that used to be the front door. "I feel like I'm strangling her."

"Impossible, Zack. Zombies are already dead,

so that means their respiratory and all of their other systems have totally stopped functioning. Except, of course, the brain, which obviously has now become its own flesh-eating impulse machine."

"Rice, lift her feet up," Zack ordered, tugging her onto the lawn. "I don't want her head to pop off."

"Whatever," Rice said, grabbing Zoe by the ankles. "But then I gotta go grab some stuff."

Zack and Rice loaded Zoe into the back of the Volvo behind the dog partition and slammed the rear door. Twinkles flattened his ears back and growled in Zoe's hideous face. Madison rocked Twinkles back and forth like a newborn baby.

In the back of the garage, Rice and Zack each picked up a T-shirt from the pile of dirty laundry and started to change.

"Don't look at us, Madison!" Rice shouted.

"*Okay*, Rice! I'll *try* not to look," Madison shouted with her back already turned.

With a fresh shirt from the dirty laundry, Rice selected a small arsenal of blunt hand weapons: a shovel, a steel crowbar, a sledgehammer, and an aluminum baseball bat. "C'mon, Zack, help me carry these." Rice picked up the crowbar and the aluminum bat.

Doodle-ee-doodle-ee-doodle-ee-doooo! A ringtone jingled from inside his backpack. "Wait." Rice turned his back around toward Zack. "I'm getting a phone call. Reach in and get it."

"Rice, you had a phone this whole time and you didn't say anything?" Madison shouted.

"Who were you gonna call? Zombie Busters?"

Zack unzipped the bag and stuck his hand inside, pulling out the Ziploc bag of zombie fingertips.

"Dude, why did you collect these things?"

"Specimens, man."

"How do you turn this thing on?" Zack handed the phone to Rice.

"Like this," Rice said. He slid his finger across the touch screen, and Zack could hear Rice's mom on the other end of the phone. "Rice, honey?"

Rice put the phone up to his ear. "Hi, Mom . . . I thought you and Dad were zombies. . . . Where are you guys? You're still at parent-teacher night? Locked in the gymnasium? That sucks. . . . Sorry, Mom, I know you don't like me using that word. Ummm, we're okay. . . . I'm fine, Mom. . . . Okay, Mom . . . I love you, too." Rice handed the phone to Zack. "Your mom wants to talk to you."

"Mom?" Zack said. "I love you, too, Mom. I know, Mom. . . . Zoe? She's busy. . . . Yeah, she's in the car. . . . Mom, we gotta hit the road. . . . Tucson . . . The Volvo . . . Calm down, Mom, Madison's driving. . . . Mom, stop yelling. . . . It's okay, Mom, we have to go. . . . I love you, too. . . . Oh, Mom, wait. . . . Don't eat any of that BurgerDog crud, I mean stuff, sorry. . . . Just don't!" Zack pressed the end button and handed the phone back to Rice.

They dragged their assortment of weapons to the car, tossing them into the back with zombie Zoe. They finished loading the Volvo and buckled up, screeching off. A few minutes later, Madison stopped at a cross street and paused.

"How do you get to the highway from here?" she asked Zack.

"I don't know," Zack said innocently. "My mom always drives me."

"Well, I don't know your neighborhood that well," Madison said, drumming the wheel with her pointer fingers.

"Don't look at me," Rice said. "I don't get out that much."

Madison peered up through the windshield. "O-M-G!" she said, pronouncing each letter deliberately.

Perched on the rooftop of a redbrick house, a cowering figure huddled in a ball, whimpering into his elbows. The man-boy lifted his head. Zack recognized his chiseled features and loveless eyes. Rice cringed.

Greg Bansal-Jones.

CHAPTER

Greg Bansal-Jones could best be classified as an eighth-grade super jock and a world-class bully. He looked at least two years older than his actual age of thirteen and three-quarters and probably went through a can of shaving cream nearly every week. Standing almost five feet nine inches tall, Greg was broad-shouldered, with an upper body of solid muscle. He was the captain of the soccer, hockey, and lacrosse teams and could totally kick Zack's butt. And Rice's butt. And more than likely both their butts at once.

"Bansal-Jones?" Rice half-whined, half-gulped. "Madison, the guy's barely a caveman. . . . He's a king-size knuckle-dragger."

"Okay, he's sort of a meathead, but he's so cute and helpless up there all shaking and pathetic. And anyway, we could use a little brute strength on our side for once. We'll be the brains and he'll be the brawn."

Zack hated Greg, not only for being so mean, but for being so spectacularly good at being so mean. Even without Rice's bathroom swirly episode, Greg had an impressive highlight reel of torments that any practicing bully would envy. Tripping a lonely fifth grader carrying a lunch tray. Checking an obese seventh-grade girl into a locker. Laughing, stamping his feet in the general vicinity of a substitute teacher searching for her lost contact lens. Straddling a sixth-grade weakling, pinching his nose, and funneling atomic hot sauce into his mouth. The list could go on forever.

"I'm not taking no for an answer," Madison told them.

Zack looked up and sighed. Rice scooted across

the backseat, curbside, buzzed down the window, and whispered to Zack: "Don't worry, man. I'm about to go medieval on this kid. . . ." And with that, Rice stuck his pink pockmarked head outside.

"Hark, young squire! I do desire we may be better strangers, you and I, but milady requests the pleasure of your company," he called up to Greg in his best British accent. "Come off your roost and join us hither."

Greg's head shot up in a welter of blubbering snot. "My mom tried to eat me!" he said, sniffling up his tears.

"Quit your sniveling!" Rice commanded. "There are droves of savage beasts on the gander. No time for mollycoddling, you flop-eared knave! Get down hence!"

"Why is he talking like that?" Madison asked Zack.

"Mrs. Rice takes him to these Renaissance festivals in the summertime. It's really weird. They all dress up in costumes and talk like they're in the Middle Ages."

"Greg barely understands regular English," Madison said.

"I think that's the point," Zack said.

"Don't tarry now, boy." Rice continued heckling like a court jester.

More than a little befuddled, Greg obliged, shimmying nimbly down the gutter that ran up the house. He landed on the lawn and jogged toward the Volvo, a red gym sack slung over his shoulder. He was still decked out in his soccer gear: shorts, shin guards, cleats, and jersey, lucky number thirteen.

"I'm so glad you're here, Mad," Greg said when he reached the car. "Who are these nerd-bombers?"

"This is Zoe's little brother, Zack. And this is his best friend, Rice," Madison introduced her partners-in-slime.

"You flushed my head in a toilet bowl about a month ago," Rice reminded him.

"Oh yeah, I remember you." Greg chuckled. "But you look different . . . your face. It's all disgusting. He's not turning into one of those things, is he?"

"No, it's just chicken pox," Madison said. "But Zoe's in the back, and she's a full-out zombie. We're gonna save her, though."

"You got Zoe back there?" Greg said curiously, moving to the rear of the car.

He cupped his hands over the back window and peered inside. Zoe huffed through the window steam and growled hideously at Greg. She bashed her lacrosse helmet against the glass, knocking him back on his heels. He tripped over the curb and fell on the grass behind him. "Oh snap, she's busted!" he shouted, popping back up.

Madison turned to Zack. "Get in the backseat."

"No way," Zack protested. "This is *my* car."

"I don't see your name on it, bro," Greg said, opening the passenger door. "Unless your last name is Volvo." Pause. "Is your last name Volvo, bro?"

Zack just sat and stared.

"Don't be difficult, Zack," Madison pleaded. "Just sit in the back with Rice."

Reluctantly, Zack surrendered his seat and stepped out of the Volvo, shoving the open door into Greg's dominating sneer.

"Hey, take it easy, dweebo," Greg taunted.

Now fully recovered from his splubbering rooftop sob show, Greg took shotgun next to Madison and gave her a wink and a smile. Twinkles skittered to the backseat and jumped up in between Zack and Rice. The little dog sighed, plunking down on the seat cushion.

"Greg, did you see which way the zombies went?" Rice asked him excitedly, like an enthusiastic dog trainer would a well-trained collie.

Greg pointed straight ahead and let out a short Neolithic grunt. Then he opened his gym bag and pulled out a grease-soaked BurgerDog takeout bag. The smell of fast food filled the car. Madison placed two fingers over her lips and puffed out her cheeks like she was going to hurl.

They followed the side street until they saw the ramp to the expressway. Greg unwrapped the BurgerDog sandwich and laid it out neatly on his lap.

"Greg, I swear if you take even one bite of that thing . . ." Madison recoiled.

"No," Rice said, mirror-tapping his fingertips like a delighted super-villain. "Let him eat. . . ."

Man, Zack thought. *I would freakin' love to see Bansal-Jones bite the big one on his sandwich. But what if the meathead actually turned into a zombie? He'd rip us apart. Then again, it'd be okay to whack him over the head with the shovel.*

Greg took the top bun off the BurgerDog. "This is the good stuff."

But it wasn't the good stuff. No, certainly not. In the low light of the car, Zack and Rice both gasped at the revolting hot dog patty burger coated with its creamy lime green special sauce, wilted lettuce, and rubbery purple onion. Underneath the goopy extras, they watched in revulsion as the meat pulsated, bubbling as if it were alive.

"See?" Greg replaced the bun and opened his mouth, ready to chomp.

"Stop!" Madison snatched the zombie burger away from Greg. "Don't eat that!"

"Why not?" Greg asked.

"Yeah, Madison . . ." Rice was disappointed. "Why not?"

"Are you crazy? The last thing we need is another zombie on our hands. Look at this thing!" she yelled, holding up the sandwich. "It's got a life of its own." Madison put down her window and prepared to chuck it to the pavement.

"Stop!" Rice yelled. He grabbed Madison's wrist from behind and pried loose the throbbing sandwich. "We may need this for a specimen. Just to be sure. I'll put it in my backpack."

Rice pulled out the bag of zombie fingers while holding the BurgerDog. Twinkles's nose twitched from side to side. The hungry pup bounded off the backseat and nipped at the infectious meat patty. Rice whapped Twinkles on the nose, and the little dog cowered back on the seat, licking its chops.

"Dude . . ." Zack whispered. He pointed at Twinkles, then at BurgerDog, then back at Twinkles again.

"Ssshhh!" Rice whispered. "Only people can turn into zombies. I read it online."

Greg crumpled the wrapper and tossed it out the window.

Madison revved the engine and cruised toward the highway entrance, dappled with clueless ghouls. Her confidence behind the wheel reached an all-time high as she steered the car coolly through the sparse cluster of walking corpses.

They sped up the on-ramp and leveled out onto the skyway, which wrapped southbound around downtown Phoenix. The Volvo shuttled down the long stretch of gray desert highway, as Zombieville, USA, grew smaller behind them. Madison accelerated, whipping by four more hulking fiends. They growled at the passing Volvo like a crazed gang of undead hitchhikers looking for a lift.

The tires whizzed along the freeway.

Outside the car, the midnight sky was a menacing gunmetal black. Moonlit mountain ranges sprang off the horizon. Coyotes howled ominously from the fringes of nowhere. This was desert country, but Zack knew that skulking in the scrub brush, there were probably hundreds of unseen zombies camouflaged under the canopy of night's shade.

Zack felt his sister's hot zombie breath puffing on the back of his neck. He gave her a look that meant "stop it," but it was no use. *She doesn't understand anything,* Zack thought. *She never did, even when she was human.* To his left, Rice's eyes were glazed over as he zoned out the side window. Zack watched his fat little friend pick the crusty scabs spackling his forearms and then jam the very same finger in his nostril, digging away obliviously. Twinkles panted quickly, fast asleep between them.

Zack settled into the lull of the car ride. The digital clock read 12:22 A.M., and the Volvo was dead quiet. Zack's lids felt heavy. Deprived of the constant squabbling, Zack drifted to sleep to the hum of the motor. He woke up a minute later, yawning. The clock read 1:23 A.M. *Was it really almost one thirty in the morning?*

On went the Volvo, rolling along swiftly. The headlights beamed through the darkness, illuminating the white dash marks scurrying toward them under the hood of the car. Greg was talking to Madison up front.

"How'd you end up with these scrubs anyway, Mad?" Greg said.

"I was sleeping over at Zoe's. How'd you end up on that roof?" she asked.

"Uh . . . I climbed, duh-uh," Greg said.

"After his mom tried to eat him," Rice reminded anyone who had forgotten.

"I'd stop talking if I were you," Greg threatened.

"I'm not scared of you, Greg," Rice countered.

"You wanna get your face flushed again, Poop Boy? Cuz this time, I'll make you lick the bowl," Greg warned. Rice gulped.

"Leave him alone, Greg!" Zack yelled.

"Who are you again?" Greg asked, exasperated. "I've never even seen you before."

"Zoe's brother." Madison knocked on his head, which made a hollow sound.

They were now speeding up over a hill, easily going seventy miles per hour, when suddenly it appeared: a winding caravan of ticking red taillights flickering not too far up ahead. The other cars were at a complete standstill, but the Volvo kept picking up momentum as they hurtled headlong down the steep slope.

"Madison, slow down!" Zack shouted, starting to panic. The flashing taillights doubled nearer—bumper to bumper to bumper.

"Umm," Rice said. "We're gonna need to start stopping, like, now!"

Madison pressed the brakes, but the Volvo was fast approaching the traffic jam. Greg held on to the grab-handle above the door, grinning like a wide-eyed thrill-seeker on a screaming roller coaster.

"Now, Madison!" Zack screamed.

"I am, Zack!" Madison yelled back.

"Press harder!"

She smashed the pedal, and the car began to rumble and grind. The rear of the backed-up traffic was so close that Zack began to think they couldn't possibly stop in time. He shut his eyes tightly, but all he could picture was his mom's Volvo blasting into the wall of cars.

The tires ground into the slanted pavement. Madison floored the brakes. Rice crossed his heart and hoped not to die. Zack watched the collision happen over and over on the backs of his eyelids.

As they dipped back up from the downward tilt, the car jerked to a stop, and zombie Zoe rammed full force into the partition, clanking the metal bars of her face mask against the iron-mesh cage. Everyone shot forward, bruising their collarbones on tightening seat belts. Everyone that is, except for Twinkles, whose teensy frame went sailing sharply into the front console and turned on the radio.

"Omigosh! Twinkle-face!" Madison scooped him up with one hand.

The same beeping alert signal pierced their stunned silence. They heard the same robotic voice as before, announcing updates over the system: "Security checkpoints have been set up between cities to prevent illegal zombie crossing. Police searches will be conducted on every vehicle. Law enforcement and military personnel will be working together to contain the spreading zombie epidemic. Any undead passengers will be terminated on sight. The cause of the outbreak is still unknown."

"What was that all about?" Madison asked.

"It means that if we wait here and they find Zoe, then it's bye-bye Zoe," Rice answered, concealing his glee. "Geez, Zack. I told you we shouldn't have brought her along!"

"But . . ." Madison sounded completely baffled. "They can't just kill them, can they?"

About ten cars ahead of them, two mustachioed Arizona state troopers sauntered down the endless line of packed traffic. They were accompanied by two huge droopy basset hounds, sniffing at attention. The patrolmen shined their flashlights inside the car, questioning the passengers. They checked the backseat and then ordered the driver to open the trunk.

"They're checking every single car!" Zack said, distraught.

"What are we going to do?" Madison asked nervously.

Suddenly, the troopers jumped back and reached

for their holsters. An old lady shot up out of the trunk. The driver of the car threw himself in front of his undead mother, blocking her from the trigger-happy cops. The old zombified lady attacked the driver, biting him on his shoulder.

"Yo!" Rice shouted.

"Sweet," Greg said.

"We've got to get off this road pronto." Zack wondered how it would feel if he were an only child.

"Do you see any other roads, genius?" Madison asked in a panic.

"There's a gate right there." Rice pointed east. An open metal gateway marked a dirt road, which ran from the highway over a small ditch into the desert. "It could be a shortcut."

"You want us to go off-roading in a Volvo?" Greg asked.

"You got a better idea?"

Greg didn't respond.

"That's what I thought," Rice said, addressing Madison now. "Kill the headlights. I'll use my iPhone to navigate us through the back roads."

"Assuming there are even any roads back there," Zack said glumly.

Rice opened his bag, rummaging around. The zombie fingers wiggled around next to the BurgerDog. "Here it is." Rice pulled out the phone. "Full steam ahead."

Madison steered the Volvo off the highway and onto the gravel path. The headlights went dark, and the phantom Volvo crept into the twittering hush of the desert.

CHAPTER

The Volvo crunched onward over the gritty unpaved road, spraying a cloud of rocky dust behind them. Rice palmed his phone, awaiting the exact directions for the military outpost, but the device was stalling. Over and over again, the message flashed across the screen: *Network busy.*

"Just keep going straight," he instructed.

"At this point, I don't think we have any other choice," Madison said anxiously.

"Don't worry," Rice assured them. "We'll get there."

The moon broke through the clouds momentarily, and a dim glow flared over the cactus fields. Squinting out the side window, Zack could barely make out three

highlighted figures, kneeling in the dirt, jamming their bloated, lumpy hands into their faces like three gluttons devouring a bucket of chicken wings.

As the Volvo advanced everyone saw the trio of zombie cannibals.

"They're feeding," Rice observed.

"Change the subject!" Madison demanded. "I don't even want to talk about what that was."

Zack held Twinkles on his lap, petting the traumatized puppy until Twinkles's eyes closed and he dozed off again.

"Madison," Zack said, worried, "Twinkles isn't looking so good."

"What's wrong with him?" she asked.

"I don't know. He's breathing kind of funny."

Twinkles slept, purring out little growls between wheezy breaths.

"He's fine," Madison said. "Just let him sleep."

Rice smacked the phone into the butt of his hand. "What's wrong with this stupid thing?" he cursed.

"It stinks in here," Madison mumbled, fanning the air in front of her face. "That's what's wrong." The Volvo was filled with an unbearable combination of the BurgerDog fumes leaking from Rice's bag and Zoe's pungent funk of rot and decay.

Zack felt like he could reach out and touch the toxic stench. Inhaling through his mouth, he felt the thick syrupy odor melt on his tongue and become a flavor.

Madison put down her window and gasped, sucking in a great big helping of fresh air. Zack, Rice, and Greg did the same. "Rice, if you don't figure that thing out really, really soon, I'm really, really turning around."

"And then the cops will really, really blow Zoe's brains out," Rice said. "Is that what you want?"

"Of course not. We'll just explain to them that she's with us and then—"

Zombie Zoe snapped and snarled, butting her helmet continuously into the metal barrier.

"The cops will blow her brains out," he repeated slowly, shaping his index finger and thumb like a pistol and pointing it at his temple. "Bang."

"Rice! I refuse to keep driving when we don't even know if this road will take us anywhere," Madison complained.

"She's got a point, bro," Greg snipped.

"I'm sure she does, *bro*," Rice countered. "Do you?"

"How about if I give you one on top of your fat head?"

"Yeah, whatever, *Greg.* . . ." Rice looked down at the phone. "Hold on, you guys. Here we go. There's gonna be another road in point three miles. We make a right, and that will take us directly to the Tucson Air Force Base!"

"Finally!"

"It's about time."

"Rice, that's awesome, man," Zack said.

"Just kidding, guys." Rice started to crack up. "I have no freaking clue where we are. . . ." He paused, trapped in a silent full-on belly chuckle.

Greg twisted around in his seat and yanked the phone easily from Rice's pudgy mitts.

Rice let out a pitifully helpless yelp. "Hey, give that back!"

"Mine," Greg said forcefully. The bully mammoth looked at the digital screen of the iPhone. He flicked his wrist out the open window, and the phone vanished.

"Thanks, idiot," Rice said. "Now you owe my parents three hundred bucks."

"What're you gonna do about it, dork?" Greg wiggled his fist under his eye and mouthed silently, "Boo-hoo! Wah-wah!"

Zack glanced down at the slumbering pup, lying

stone still in his lap. Something wasn't right with Twinkles.

"Madison?" Zack said hesitantly. "Twinkles isn't breathing."

"What!" Madison cried. "What do you mean?"

"Your dog is dead," Greg said. Madison's right arm flew out on reflex, backhanding Greg in the face. "Owww!"

"What are you, some kind of doctor?" she cried.

Zack cupped the lifeless puppy snugly in his hands. Madison's concerned face softened into sorrow. A lone tear twinkled in the corner of her eye and rolled down her cheek. Twinkles was gone.

"Can't you give him CPR or something?" Madison wept.

"Yo, I used to be a lifeguard at the summer day camp," Greg spoke up. "We all had to learn mouth-to-mouth in case some loser forgot how to swim, but I'm not kissing that dog on the mouth."

"Yes, you are," Madison ordered. "Zack, give Twinkles to Greg, now!"

"Gladly," Zack passed Twinkles's limp cadaver up front.

Rice nudged Zack. "This oughta be good."

Using the dashboard like an operating table, Greg flopped Twinkles on his back and started pushing at his tiny rib cage with his pinky fingers.

"This is to keep the blood pumping to the heart," Greg explained.

"Try not to break him," Madison said. Greg lifted the puppy's muzzle, pulled down its chin, and opened its mouth, which glistened with teeny-tiny pearly white fangs.

"Now I'm going to blow air into its mouth and

inflate the lungs," Greg said. He puffed a long breath into Twinkles's open snout, then pressed the Boggle's itty-bitty chest again, counting to five. He gave the dog another breath, and Twinkles's eyes popped open.

"Look!" Madison said. "It's working." Greg gave the dog one more sequence of chest pumps and leaned in for the third round of mouth-to-snout.

All of a sudden, Twinkles lurched up off the dash and plunged his tiny fangs into Greg's bottom lip. Greg howled in pain, as the reanimated Zoggle clamped its itty-bitty teeth down deep into his kisser.

"Aaah-ha-ha . . . Aaaaaaah-ha-ha!" Greg shrieked. He grabbed the zombified puppy by the midsection, yanked hard, and ripped it from his lip in a bloodred spurt. Greg heaved the evil little creature out of the open window. Twinkles sailed, snarling, through the air, and splattered on a craggy patch of roadside bedrock. Greg's mouth poured blood.

"Greg, how could you?" Madison cried. She stopped the car and smacked Greg in the face again, then hopped out and jogged to the spot where Twinkles had landed.

"Owwwww," Greg yelped. "Stop doing that!"

At the side of the road, Madison stood over the lifeless puppy, her hands glued to her face. Zack and Rice left Greg behind in the Volvo, blotting his bloody lip with a BurgerDog napkin and wincing in the mirror on the back of the visor.

Twinkles lay motionless on the smooth beige rock. The boys stood behind Madison as she wept for her puppy. The crazed zombie grimace had vanished, and now the tiny dog just looked as though it were sleeping peacefully.

"Well, we can't just leave the poor thing lying in the middle of the desert," Madison whimpered, teary-eyed.

"You're absolutely right, Madison," Rice agreed. "Twinkles will make an excellent specimen." He reached down for the zombified dog, but Madison slapped his hand away.

"Back off, twerp," Madison cried.

"But, Madison, we have to—"

"Rice, just shut up, okay?" Zack pleaded. He knelt next to Madison as she lifted poor Twinkles off the cool flat rock and placed his body gently in her purse.

Back in the car, the mood was gloomy. Madison drove on ahead until Rice broke the silence. "Does this mean Greg is going to turn into a zombie now?" he asked. Zack said nothing, quietly rooting for the zombie virus coursing through Greg's bloodstream.

"I hope not," Greg said. "'Cuz that would not be too cool."

"You know what else isn't that cool?" Madison asked, stomping on the gas pedal. The engine revved and sputtered. Steam rose from under the hood of the Volvo, and the smell of scorched gasoline seeped in through the air vents. The fuel gauge pointed to *E*. "That we're out of gas!" she shrieked, slamming the steering wheel in frustration. *Hooooooooonnk!* The car horn blared across the zombie desert. A tortured moan swelled in the distance.

CHAPTER 15

fter a quick debate, which Madison won by decree, it was decided that Zoe would join them on foot.

"She's still family," Madison pointed out.

"Sure she is," Rice said. "The Addams family."

Greg yanked Zoe so hard by the leash that her head almost popped off. Rice gathered the assortment of hand weapons he'd chosen from the garage and passed them out accordingly: a shovel for Zack, a crowbar for Madison, a sledgehammer for Greg, and the Louisville Slugger for himself.

As they began their march into the desert, zombie

Zoe proved to be good motivation for them to keep moving at a steady pace. If they stopped, she'd be in hot pursuit, snaggletoothed inside her lacrosse helmet. And if they pushed ahead too quickly, she anchored them, like she was a bulldog being dragged on an unwanted stroll.

They walked this way for three eternal minutes before Greg opened his mouth. "Can a dog-zombie really turn people-persons into person-zombies?" he murmured.

"Hopefully," Rice said. "Then we won't have to listen to you try and think."

"One more word and you're dead meat," said Greg, pounding the heavy hammer into his open hand with ease.

"You couldn't take both of us, even with that sledgehammer," Rice said.

Speak for yourself, Zack thought. The idea of Greg attacking them *without* a weapon was terrifying enough.

"Yer kidding, right?" Greg said. "I'd mop the floor with the both of you."

"Will you guys quit your macho talk? My puppy is dead, and there's nothing we can do about it! And Rice? Greg would crush, like, fifteen of you at once."

"Not if I were zombies, he couldn't."

Zack chuckled to himself and pictured the epic battle: Bansal-Jones vs. fifteen little porky Rice gremlins. Now Greg sidled up to Madison. They walked together and held hands. Zombie Zoe brought up the rear, slobbering behind her face mask in slow, mindless pursuit.

"I'm hungry," Rice said, tapping his gut. "Aren't you hungry?"

"I haven't eaten since the food fight. And Madison ruined my cake!"

"Gimme your hand," Rice said, opening a canister of the ginkgo tablets from Albertsons. Zack shot his friend a cockeyed glance. "No, seriously, I swear I wasn't making it up." Rice tapped out a few pills into Zack's open palm, and then some into his own. "You know, I don't think I've ever been up this late before," he kept talking.

"What time is it?" Zack yawned.

"Like two thirty in the morning, I think." Rice raised his handful of ginkgo.

"You first," Zack insisted.

"Zombie garlic," Rice toasted his friend and tossed the pills down his throat.

"You two dingleberries better not have any secret snacks up there that I don't know about!" Greg barked loudly.

"Yeah," Madison said. "What are you guys eating?"

"Ginkgo biloba!" Rice called. "Want some?"

"The ginkgo doesn't do anything," she said. "We already tried it, remember?"

"Suit yourself, Madison."

As they walked onward, the underbrush thickened gradually on both sides of the road. A chorus of desert insects blurped and tweeted. With every step, the terrain grew more and more perilous, all flat stones and cacti, bloodroot and sagebrush. Ahead of them, an abandoned pickup truck flashed its hazards under a Joshua tree, which flared and dimmed in the light's slow flicker, marking the end of the checkpointless back road.

Greg and Madison caught up to the boys, who had stopped dead in their tracks.

"Graveyard . . ." Zack pointed, his index finger trembling.

It was surrounded by a black wrought-iron fence. A white stone mausoleum stood dead center, flanked by row upon row of much smaller headstones. A shovel was stabbed in a large pile of dirt beside three freshly dug grave holes.

"Come on, guys. Let's go check it out," Madison said with a renewed sense of purpose.

"I'm not so sure that's a good idea," Rice said.

"Fine." Madison slapped the end of Zoe's leash into Rice's chest. "Then it's your turn to zombie-sit." Greg snatched the baseball bat away from Rice and saddled him with the sledgehammer instead.

Madison grabbed Zack's arm, leading him toward the cemetery. "Bring the shovel. I'm not touching that other one," she added.

"Why do we need the shovel?" he asked.

"We're going to give Twinkles a proper burial," she said, dragging Zack along. The dirt road cornered sharply and wrapped around the back of the grave-yard.

"Come on, Zo," Rice said, tugging the leash toward the pickup truck, dragging the sledgehammer with dif-ficulty. "You two have fun at your funeral."

Madison hauled Zack through the open cemetery gate. Greg followed, jumping deliberately on all the graves, as they made their way into the graveyard.

"Greg, stop being so immature," Madison said.

Greg ignored her, leapfrogging over a row of stone crosses. "Yippee!"

"Dude, are you all right, Greg?" Zack asked.

"Chill, bro! I'm fine." Greg's lip looked nasty, all clotted and chunky.

"All right, be nice," said Madison, sighing. "I'm gonna go find something to use for Twinkles's tomb-stone. Then we'll hold the service. You should start digging." She left her bag with Zack and wandered to the other side of the graveyard.

Zack walked cautiously between the rows of graves. Using one of Rice's flashlights, he began to read the headstones. Before every name was the abbreviation for a specific military rank: PFC, Maj., Col., Lieut., Gen. *These are all soldiers,* he realized. *Well . . . Twinkles was a real trooper, too,* Zack thought. After scoping out the area some more, he found the perfect spot for the dog and started to dig.

Over by the pickup truck, Rice had finished tethering Zoe to a signpost. She was panting wildly, straining for Rice with outstretched arms, clasping and unclasping her hands with intent to claw. Rice whipped out some ginkgo and started firing pellets into her mouth.

He stopped and looked at the back of the truck, then called over to Zack. "Dude, this truck's got military plates and a siren! I think we might be closer to that air force base than we thought. . . ."

"Yeah, I think this is an army graveyard," Zack called back. "What does PFC stand for?"

"Private, First Class," Rice answered.

Twinkles Miller. Puppy, First Class. Zack planned out the little dog's epitaph. He glanced at the shovel protruding from the mound of soil and the three empty holes in the ground.

"Who digs graves by themselves at two in the morning?" Zack shouted.

"I don't think I want to know the answer to that question," Rice responded.

"Are the keys in the truck?" Zack asked Rice.

"Hold on," he said. "Let me check. . . ."

Zack started to dig again, keeping his eye on Greg, who had just put down the baseball bat after a rousing duel against three imaginary zombies: "Hah-ho, en garde, zombie!" Greg then wandered over to the mausoleum and picked up what seemed to be a king-size fountain soda. The wiener dog mascot winked at Zack on the side of the cup.

"Yo, someone's been eatin' BurgerDog!" Greg wrapped his lips around the straw and ripped a long noisy sip from the under-taker's flat, lukewarm backwash. "Not cool, bro. If the Gregster can't eat the Dog, then nobody can eat the Dog."

Zack began to dig faster. *What was taking Madison so long?*

Suddenly, a wet, heavy splash sounded off the marble doorstep of the tomb. Zack lifted his head and looked over toward the mausoleum. Greg was puking. Everywhere.

CHAPTER 16

Madison stepped around the corner of the towering stone vault, carrying a flat slab of desert rock. Greg heaved and stumbled toward her. Zack ditched the shovel and walked over to see what was happening.

"Argh! I'm . . . dying. . . ."

Madison backed away as the pale-faced bully bobbed and swayed before collapsing at her feet. She crouched and put her hand under the back of his head.

"Oh, Greg, what happened?" she said.

"I don't know," he coughed. "It musta been Twinker-bell. . . ." Greg was really sweating now. His eyes were puffy, heavy-lidded, struggling not to close.

"I knew it," Zack said. "Madison, back away from zombie Greg."

"He's not even dead yet," Madison said. "I'm not abandoning someone when they're on their death-bed. . . . Ick!"

Greg grunted. A snot bubble burst off his nostril and splashed the back of Madison's hand. "Eww, Zack, get over here. He's all drippy and . . . just ewww." Greg coughed, and a blob of green mucus dribbled off his chin. "Quick, it's gonna get me," Madison said, refer-ring to the trickle of Greggy slime.

"What am I supposed to do?" Zack said, kneeling down next to her.

"Hold out your hands," she instructed. Zack obeyed. "Now hold his head." And she plopped Greg's head into Zack's hands and wiped the snot off on his jeans.

"I'm not holding this kid's head," Zack said. But Zack was holding his head all right, cushioning Greg's skull ever so tenderly.

"Don't let me die, dork," Greg gasped. "We've got

a huge soccer game next Saturday. . . ." His eyes rolled back, and his body slackened.

"Oh my God, he just died. What do I do?" Zack asked, flustered.

A few moments passed, and Greg regained consciousness, still human. "Zack," he croaked, "here." Greg was holding Rice's phone. "I didn't really toss it. . . . I was gonna keep it for myself. . . . These things are sweet as H-E-double hockey sticks. . . ." Greg passed out again.

Zack stood up and placed the phone in his pants pocket. He lifted Greg under his knees at the top of his soccer socks. "Come on, Madison," he said. "We gotta get him tied up before he changes into a zombie. Grab his wrists."

Greg's body swung heavily between them as they shimmied past the tomb. Struggling and straining with his weight, Madison dropped Greg's arms, and his head hit the dirt with a thud.

"I need a break," she said, dust-clapping her hands.

"Not now, Madison!" Zack urged. "Come on." They started to lift the unconscious lug and nearly buckled under the massive strain of Bansal-Jones's deadweight. Just then, Zack's jaw dropped to the soil along with Greg's heels as a huge menacing shadow appeared out of nowhere, darkening their path.

"Hey, I thought we weren't taking breaks," Madison said. But when she saw Zack's face, she turned and dropped her half of Greg's carcass. *WHUMP!*

It looked like an absolute sideshow freak, six and a half feet of decaying zombie flesh. It was wearing some

kind of industrial blue jumpsuit, the left breast embroidered with the name LONGLY.

Longly's face had more or less collapsed, slumping down the cheekbones in an avalanche of muck. A heaping cluster of bulbous lumps was growing off the side of his bald head. His mouth hung open, drooping jaws unhinged, flashing a mouthful of yellow pointed daggers. He lunged.

Madison shrieked and fell backward, scrambling in place. The butts of her hands and the heels of her shoes dug in the loose dirt and then slipped, going nowhere in a puff of dust.

The deformed, moldering colossus folded in a quick spasm of rigor mortis and clamped his meathooks around Madison's ankle. Eclipsed by the zombie's wide, black shadow, Madison kicked, frantic to get away, but the great zombie brute was too powerful.

Now acting on pure impulse, Zack launched Twinkles's soon-to-be headstone through the air like a Frisbee. It slammed hard against the zombie's head, and the diseased undertaker wrenched around, bellowing. Madison twisted free of the creature's clutches.

Zack picked up the baseball bat, gripping it tightly, and circled around the enormous zombie gravedigger. He swung hard and drove the top of the bat into the monster's hip. But it just kept coming, swiping madly for Zack's tasty little brain nugget.

He's too tall, Zack thought, unable to reach the zombie's beastly head. Zack swung again, this time connecting with its knee, thinking that perhaps he might chop the thing down to a more manageable size. He longed for the ax lying idly on the garage floor.

Next, Zack gave the zombie giant's midsection a good whack and heard its innards slosh around inside of its belly.

"Hit it on the head, Zack!" Madison yelled.

"I'm trying!"

Suddenly, the towering undertaker pounced jerkily, mere inches from wringing Zack's pencil neck with its giant, knotted hands. But Zack was too quick and dove between its bumbling legs.

Zack bounded up the marble steps and hopped onto the stone banister of the mausoleum. The undead monster spun around and grunted in confusion. But Zack was already in position, looming well above the gigantic zombie, the bat cocked back straight over his head.

"Now you see me," Zack said, allowing the zombie to turn around and give him one final look. "And now you don't."

WHAM! Zack brought down the Slugger on top of the zombie's skull as hard as he could. The zombie swooned and crumpled in a heap of dislocated bones and flayed bubbly skin.

"Way to go, Zachar-ee!" Madison cheered. They were both so excited that they failed to notice what was happening right beside them. . . .

Greg was waking up.

CHAPTER

Zack jumped down and stepped on the defeated zombie's chest. He threw his arms up victoriously, but then quickly backed away. One blow to the head was little more than a catnap for this thing, and Zack had no idea when it might wake up.

Across the graveyard, Rice broke into a sprint. He ran as fast as his short little legs would carry him, flailing his arms and pointing.

While Madison clapped cheerfully for Zack Clarke, zombie chaser, Greg's torso lifted straight off the ground, stiff as a board. His bent, shadowy outline jerked forward.

"Madison!" Zack yelled. "Behind you!"

Zombie Greg's cold dead fingers curled around her calf, and Madison tried to leap away. But the zombie super jock's viselike grip was unshakable.

"Help! I can't budge!" Madison screamed,

Zombie Greg wrenched his head back and swung his neck to one side. Rice flung himself at Greg and dropped his shoulder into the reanimated psycho-jock. But Rice was no match for the Gregster's brute strength. Rice bounced off zombie Greg, who clamped his toothy mug onto the back of Madison's leg and bit down hard.

"Ooowwwwwww!" she wailed, and dropped to the ground. Greg whipped his head from side to side like a dog playing tug on a chew toy. He snarled and chewed.

Zack reached the bloody fray and swung the bat hard, clocking zombie Greg in the temple. Bansal-Jones slumped to the ground. Too little, too late. Madison had been bitten, and the superb delight of clubbing Greg over the head was now only bittersweet. Madison sobbed in the dirt, her leg bearing a gnarly red gash. Rice was rubbing his head, dizzy from the spill.

"Come on, Rice," Zack said. "Help me get her out of here." They raised Madison, who wobbled on one good leg, stunned and shaking. She draped her arms around their shoulders, and they limped a safe distance before Madison collapsed. She sprawled out on the ground between them, her knee bent and her leg dripping blood.

"Dang, Madison, your leg looks raunchy!" said Rice.

"Don't you have some bandages or something in that backpack of yours?" Zack asked.

"Maybe I do and maybe I don't."

"Well? Do you or don't you?"

"Of course I do. But she's just gonna turn into one of them, Zack! It'd be a waste of a good bandage. . . . Soon she'll be the enemy. Remember Twinkles?"

Madison's eyes shimmered with tears, but she bit her lip and breathed deeply, trying to accept the immense pain in her leg.

"Rice," Zack said. "If you don't start bandaging her leg in the next ten seconds, I'm gonna tell her your secret shame."

"But you swore a blood oath that you would never tell another living soul."

"According to you, she's not a living soul. She might as well be a zombie, remember? Madison, would you like to know Rice's secret . . . ?"

"Fine, fine, fine," Rice conceded.

"Zack," Madison said, coughing pathetically as he wrapped her leg with gauze, "can you get my bag for me? I'm so parched, I just want a sip of something."

"Sure," Zack said.

He ran over to the unfinished hole he'd begun to

carve out for Twinkles. He picked up the purse, for-getting its contents, and strained with the unexpected weight of it. He pulled out the crowbar and tossed it on the ground. He reached back in the bag and felt Twinkles's rigid body, sopping wet with VitalVegan-PowerPunch. Zack pulled out the soaked puppy and laid it on its side next to the half-dug grave. Twinkles's fur was stained pink from the fruity beverage, which had leaked all over the inside of Madison's purse.

Zack brought the bag over to Madison, who poked her bandage and winced in pain. He handed her the half-empty bottle.

"There's no use denying it," she said. "If it weren't for that dog, I'd never have been bitten in the first place. Now I'm gonna turn into a zombie just like everyone else. I'll be ugly and hideous and stinky." She took a sip of the lukewarm drink.

"Okay, I hate to say this, but since you're going to change into a zombie, we'd better tie you up so we don't have to worry when you come back to life," Rice announced matter-of-factly.

"Can't we just wait until she passes out?" Zack asked.

"No, Zack, he's right," Madison said. "It's the smart thing to do. I don't want to bite one of you guys and infect you, too."

Once again, Madison went into her handbag and pulled out the infamous duct tape. "This will work," she said. "We already tested it on Zack."

"Ha-ha. Real funny." Zack snorted sarcastically.

Rice stretched out the tape and bound Madison's ankles together. Having finished the feet, he looked up and said, "All right. Now gimme yer hands."

"Not yet," she said, extracting a compact mirror from her bag. "I have to say good-bye to someone first."

She clicked open the compact and stared at her reflection. Zack and Rice exchanged uncertain looks.

"Well, face, we've had some pretty awesome times. I can't believe it's over so soon."

Rice leaned over and whispered to Zack as Madison said farewell to each one of her facial features individually.

"Is this normal?" Rice asked.

"I don't really know," Zack said. "She is pretty conceited."

"Yeah, but Greg started acting kind of demented just before he went zombie."

"That's a good point."

"Goodbye, chin . . ." Madison finished her valediction to her face and frowned, pouting her lips and raising her eyebrows.

CHAPTER

e're not taking any chances." Rice said. "Time to tape up those hands, Madison."

"Not too tight, Rice." Madison held out her wrists.

Zack walked away, kicking the dirt. "What are we going to do now?" he asked. "We're stranded, and probably doomed to become zombies, too."

"We're not stranded," Rice said, pointing to the truck.

"Oh yeah, I forgot we have a truck that we don't have the keys to. And even if we did, we couldn't drive it 'cuz we're too freakin' short. Face it, Rice. We're toast."

"Oh, quit your whining, you big baby," Rice said, puffing out his chest. "First we go take care of zombie Greg and then we gotta find those keys." He snatched the duct tape and snagged the line of rope attached to his pack.

They jogged over to where zombie Greg lay on the ground in a contorted slump. "He looks like the same old Greg, doesn't he?" Zack asked. Except for a few open sores around his forehead and under his eye, Greg looked relatively normal.

"I guess so," Rice said. "But give him a chance to really zombify." They bent down and sorted out the sideways corpse till Greg's body was flat on its back. "This would be so much easier if you had just brained him."

"I couldn't do that," Zack said.

"I know, the vegan would have freaked," Rice said. "And besides, Greg will make a great specimen."

"All right, Rice," said Zack, picking up Greg's legs. "Wrap him up."

Rice cranked the duct tape around and around. Next they taped Greg's knees, then finished with the wrists.

"Nice work," Zack said. Now they turned around to

face the mausoleum, and Rice scoped out the massive fallen creature for the first time.

"That is one magnificent zombie, dude," Rice proclaimed.

"Those keys have to be on him somewhere." Zack stepped up and poked the zombie with the baseball bat, rocking it slightly. He heard the metallic jangle of a key chain. Underneath the hip of the sleeping monster, the key ring was fastened to a belt loop. "There," Zack cried. "Reach under and get them!"

"No way," Rice said. "I'm not touching that thing bare-handed. I could have microscopic cuts on my hand, and then the slime could infect me —"

"Hurry!" Zack said. "Before he wakes up!" He shoved the baseball bat underneath the zombie and lifted the handle upward so that Rice could reach the belt loop.

Rice wormed his hands under the swampy, diseased flesh and unhooked the keys, grimacing the whole time.

"Okay, got 'em." Rice gagged, diving away with a jangly clink. He stood up and whipped the key chain at his friend. "You happy now?" The Louisville Slugger was now gloppy with zombie pus, and Zack whipped a glob in Rice's direction.

"I hope you're satisfied," Rice said, and wiped his hand on Zack's shirt.

"Whatever, man, let's just take care of Greg and get out of here."

They stooped over zombie Greg, and Zack wiped the Slugger clean on Greg's soccer jersey.

"Shoot, how are we gonna carry him?" Zack asked.

"Here," Rice said, and uncoiled the rope. He threaded it between Greg's duct-taped legs, up the length of his front, and out through the sticky wrist-cuffs taped above his head. Rice took one end of the rope and handed the other to Zack, who wrapped it around his hand and held the aluminum bat firmly.

Side by side, the two friends dragged zombie Greg back toward Madison, whom Zack fully expected to be zombifying.

"You got the keys, right?" Rice asked.

"Yeah . . . but how are we supposed to drive without Madison?"

"I don't know, man. We'll figure it out."

From the far end of the cemetery, Madison sat up and called to them. "You guys are taking forever," she said.

"Do you feel like a zombie yet?" Rice grunted. "I kind of want to get out of here."

"No . . . I feel like taking off this tape, though," she said. "It's really uncomfortable." She tried to break free from her duct-tape manacles.

"Sorry, Madison," Rice huffed. "No can do. Too risky. But don't worry, you'll be a zombie soon and then you won't even care."

Zack and Rice dropped the rope and bent over, huffing and puffing. Rice's eyes zeroed in on Madison's final swig of kiwi-strawberry vegan juice. He waddled over and picked up the bottle.

"Rice, don't drink that!" Madison screamed. "It's my last sip ever," she whimpered.

He twisted off the cap and sniffed. "Ooh, kiwi-strawberry . . ." he said, tormenting her.

"Rice, please," Madison begged. "I'm dying over here!"

"So am I!" he retorted. "Do you know how heavy that kid is?"

"Pretty please with zombies on top. That's my all-time favorite drink, and it's my last sip forever and ever!"

"What is this stuff anyway?"

"It's magically delicious," she said pathetically.

Rice furrowed his eyebrows, reading the label. "How much of this junk do you drink?"

"I don't know, like five or six bottles a day?" she answered. And then without hesitating, Rice tipped his head back and gulped the final swig.

"Rice!" she yelled. "That was the meanest thing you've ever done!" She scowled.

"Oh, quit your mean-muggin'," Rice said. "I was thirsty, and besides . . ."

"That was pretty mean, dude," Zack interrupted, siding with Madison. "I mean, it was her dying wish—"

"No, it wasn't," Rice said. "Because that's not going to be her last sip!"

"What are you talking about?" Zack asked.

Rice cleared his throat, then recited like an old-time medicine man selling his patented magic elixir: "All-natural, high-energy, organic fruit drink supplement. Fortified with blah, blah, blah . . . and *ginkgo biloba* to boost your brain and your body."

Rice threw the empty bottle into the air and jumped a miraculous two inches off the dirt. "Don't you see? She's been drinking so much of this stuff that it's rendered her immune."

"Don't get my hopes up, Rice," Madison said.

"Remember what happened last time you tried out your ginkgo theory?"

"But that was different, Madison. I'm not trying to squirt you with ginkgo water. I don't have to. You can't turn into a zombie. I mean, sure, they could still rip you limb from limb, but you're un-zombie-fiable because of the ginkgo! I told you it would work." Rice placed his hands on his hips proudly and cocked his chin up.

"Wait a second," Zack said. "You don't know that for sure."

"Think about it, Zack. She's a pure ginkgo vegan, man! She probably doesn't even eat honey because one bee died to make it."

Madison nodded. "He's right. I don't."

"She's the complete opposite of everything that's going on! The zombies . . . the BurgerDog . . . everything!"

They all paused, contemplating the notion. Then, in a mad dash to the backpack, the boys busted out the ginkgo, gobbling pills by the mouthful.

"This maybe wasn't such a great idea," Zack said, spitting out the bitter powder.

"I have a better idea," Rice said. He brought over a bottle of ginkgo to Greg's lifeless corpse and knelt down. Rice began stuffing ginkgo capsules into Greg's mouth. "Help me, Zack. He's not swallowing."

"What do you want me to do?" Zack said, crouching down next to Greg.

"Ummm, try closing his mouth and plugging his nose."

"That won't work," Zack said. "He's not even breathing."

"Well, then just stuff them down his throat or some-thing."

"I'm not putting my fingers in his mouth!"

"It's your turn, man. I shoved my hand underneath that nasty thing over there!"

"Fine," Zack groaned. He closed his eyes and jammed his fingers deep down Bansal-Jones's throat. He felt a chunk of vomit in his own throat and shuddered. "There. Done."

"Good work, buddy," Rice said.

"Are you guys going to untie me or what?" Madison shouted impatiently.

Zack took out his Swiss Army knife and cut her free.

She rubbed her wrists and stretched her leg, grimacing from the sharp sting in her half-eaten calf muscle.

"Are you gonna be okay to drive, Madison?"

"I think so," she said, straightening her knee. "Oww . . . once I get to the truck."

"C'mon," Rice said, gathering up the scattered gear. "Let's load up and hit the road. We got to get her to the military base, pronto. She could be the answer to the outbreak!"

"What about Twinkles?" Madison asked with puppy dog eyes. "He hasn't had a proper burial."

"No time for burials, Madison," Rice answered, zipping up his pack.

"Dude," Zack said.

"What?" Rice whined, eyes wide and palms up.

"It's the right thing to do."

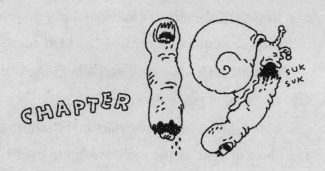

CHAPTER 19

"Wait," Madison said, sniffling. "Where's the headstone?"

"Oh, shoot!" Zack exclaimed, knocking his forehead. "It's over there!" He pointed to the fallen giant still unconscious in front of the tomb.

"Umm, I don't think we're gonna need it anymore," Rice pointed to Twinkles's unfinished grave.

Twinkles was whirling around and around, chomping his own tail.

"Twinkles is alive!" Madison limped over to her precious pup. She reached down. He growled and latched onto her hand with his tiny teeth. "Owwwwww!" she howled, and flung the puppy to the ground.

"I hate to break it to you, Madison, but that is one zombified dog," said Rice.

"Are you sure?" Madison asked hopefully. "Maybe he just thought I was a treat?"

"Yeah, right," Zack said. "And Greg's lip was a snack?"

"The good news is, you're immune," Rice added.

"But *we're* not," Zack reminded him. He dumped out Madison's handbag and crept up bravely behind the zombie pup. Twinkles was so busy trying to eat himself that Zack had no trouble pouncing on the crazed animal. He zipped up Madison's purse and the little dog wriggled around inside.

"Are we good and ready now?" Rice asked with a sigh. Madison and Zack nodded in agreement. And with that, Zack and Rice dragged zombie Greg by the rope, and Madison gimped along beside

them with the captured pooch slung over her shoulder.

When they got to the truck, Zoe was slouched on the ground against the steel post of the DO NOT ENTER sign. Her eyes were open, but she was frozen in some kind of idiotic stupor, unable to move.

"She's not growling anymore," Zack observed.

"It's probably all the ginkgo I gave her," Rice offered, putting down the tailgate of the pickup. "I told you, man . . . zombie garlic."

They hoisted Greg up into the back of the truck. "How long do you think she'll stay like that?" Zack asked.

"No idea," Rice replied. "We should probably tie her up just to be safe."

Madison tossed her purse with Twinkles inside onto the small center seat cushion and boosted herself up into the driver's seat, while Zack and Rice circled zombie Zoe with the leash. They spiraled the long cord around her until she was wrapped up like a mummy.

"At least she's being cooperative for once," Rice joked. Zack cracked a smile.

"Oh, before I forget." Zack reached into his pocket.

"Greg wanted you to have this." He handed the iPhone back to its rightful owner. Rice's face lit with joy.

"Thanks, man!" Rice looked back at Greg's limp zombie corpse. "I still hate him, though."

Madison rolled down her window and stuck out her head. "Both you guys can't sit up here. My leg needs room."

"Ready?" Rice asked.

"Yup," Zack said, making a fist.

"Rock, paper, scissors, shoot!" Rice bashed his rock on Zack's scissors.

"Rock, paper, scissors, shoot!" Zack covered Rice's rock with his paper.

"Rock, paper, scissors, shoot!" Rice scissor-snipped Zack's paper.

"Yes!" Rice shouted. "Woo!" He hopped in next to Madison. They buckled up, and he handed the grave-digger's keys to Madison.

"Which way are we going?" Madison asked.

"There's only one road to take," Rice shouted.

The muffled whir of a helicopter hummed across

the sky. Rice and Madison leaned forward and peered up through the windshield. The chopper glided in the same direction as the road ahead. Its flashing lights sparkled in the night sky as the helicopter descended behind the craggy mountain peaks, not too far in the distance.

Clutching the baseball bat, Zack climbed in the back of the pickup and closed the tailgate. He crouched in between his catatonic sister and zombie Greg. "Let's go, guys! Follow that chopper!"

Madison revved the engine and accelerated. The truck surged into the night.

Not too far down the road, the headlights flashed across another sign. A wide double-posted rectangle with the words U.S. MILITARY ZONE: RESTRICTED ACCESS.

"I told you we were close!" Rice shouted back to Zack.

A mile or so down the road, the scrubland vista was replaced with a flush pine forest. The zombie moans intensified as they pushed forward through the corridor of evergreens.

All of a sudden, Greg started to choke. Zack tightened his grip on the bat, ready to deliver another knockout blow, but Greg struck first. The ginkgo capsules shot out from the back of his throat and nailed Zack in the face.

Greg opened his eyes. "I don't want to go to school today, Mom," he whined. "Mom? What's going on? Where am I? What is this?"

"Be quiet, Greg." Zack said.

"Who's Greg?"

"You are," Zack said, sliding open the little window between Madison and Rice.

"You're Greg . . ." Greg said.

"Uhhh, guys? Greg's, like, human again, but I don't think he knows who he is. Can we stop, please?"

"What do you mean Greg's human again?" Rice asked, peering into the back of the pickup.

"Stop calling me Greg!" Greg insisted.

"Okay, then what do you want to be called?"

"Not Greg," Greg replied.

"Fine," Rice said. "NotGreg it is."

"Are you going to untie me?" NotGreg asked.

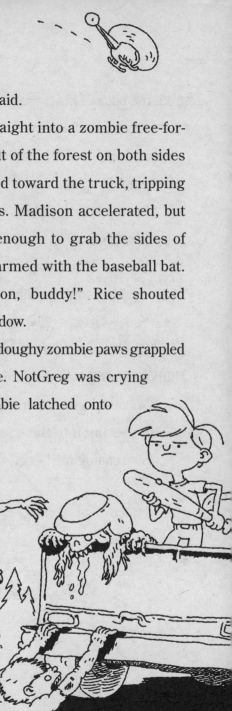

"Not a chance," Zack said.

They were driving straight into a zombie free-for-all. The undead poured out of the forest on both sides of the track. They stumbled toward the truck, tripping forward on twisted ankles. Madison accelerated, but the zombies were close enough to grab the sides of the car. Zack stood up, armed with the baseball bat.

"Don't let them on, buddy!" Rice shouted through the sliding window.

A pair of bloated, doughy zombie paws grappled at the passing vehicle. NotGreg was crying hysterically. The zombie latched onto the truck and pulled itself up, roaring psychotically and dripping pus all over NotGreg's face. Zack swung hard and felt a clunk as the bat caved in the zombie's skull like a rotten cantaloupe.

"Speed up!" Zack could see the radar towers just past the rocky foothills, where the pine forest ended but the dirt road continued. "We're almost there!"

The road tapered, narrowing at a downward slant, and they seemed to be descending underground. The truck drove under a steel entryway and rumbled into the access tunnel. The fluorescent lights overhead flickered and buzzed. All of a sudden, Madison

slammed on the brakes, and the truck screeched to a halt. The headlights beamed on a tangled knot of zombies ahead of them, blocking their path.

Madison and Rice froze with unexpected dread. Twinkles wriggled around in Madison's handbag. Zack tried to remain calm. "Madison," he said, "honk the horn." She honked twice. The zombies staggered toward them. "Now, turn on the flashers and put this bad boy in reverse."

Madison hit the switch and backed up slowly. The passageway flared and dimmed. The hideous horde of diseased fiends followed the pickup in the blinking light.

"Madison," Zack continued to direct, "keep it slow and steady. We have to lure them outside. Rice, man, you keep a head count and make sure we get all of them. Set the alarm on your phone for one minute from right now, too," Zack ordered.

"Okay . . ." Rice agreed hesitantly, and pulled out his phone.

"Set it as loud as it'll go," Zack instructed, then reached for the phone.

"Zack, what should I do?" Madison shrieked.

"We're almost out of the tunnel."

"Okay, Madison, this is important," Zack said. "You need to speed up and park out of sight. Then turn off the lights and the engine."

Madison sped up the incline in reverse and cornered around the entrance of the tunnel. The phone alarm blared in Zack's hand, and he threw it as far away from the tunnel as he could. It landed in a puff of dirt, beeping at full volume.

"Dude!" Rice whispered angrily. "That's the worst plan of all time!"

"Sshhhhhhh . . ." Zack pressed his finger to his lips.

The zombies staggered out of the tunnel, past the truck, and followed the beeping alarm in the middle of the road. As the zombies gathered around the cell phone, Madison's purse stopped growling and began to whimper instead. Rice carefully unzipped the bag, and a very confused looking, but also very puppy-looking puppy poked out his head.

"Um, guys?" Rice's eyes darted from Zack to Madison to Twinkles to NotGreg. "If this mutt's okay . . . and Bansal-Jones is okay . . . and they both bit Madison, that can only mean one thing."

"That I'm extremely lucky?" Madison asked, scooping up Twinkles.

"That you're the zombie antidote!" Rice exclaimed, a look of wonder on his face.

"Awesome! Wait. What does that mean exactly?" she asked, her brow furrowing.

"It means that if we feed you to enough zombies—"

"Not a chance, nerdbrain!" Madison sneered. "Get your own antidote."

"Okay then we'll have to clone you and let the zombies eat your clones."

Twinkles barked happily. "See, even Twinkles thinks it's a good plan."

Ruff! Ruff!

The zombies whipped their heads back around toward the truck.

"We'll figure out what that means later, but right now we gotta move!" Zack said, pointing to the zombies.

Madison flicked the headlights and started the truck. The engine sputtered and coughed. "It's not going!" Madison cried, twisting the key in the ignition over and over.

The ragged mob of zombies lumbered back toward the truck.

"Mommy, no!" NotGreg whined, and curled into a ball, clutching his knees into his chest.

"C'mon, Madison!" Zack and Rice shouted.

"Don't die on us now!" Madison pleaded, turning the key again.

At the head of the undead pack, the zombie nearest the pickup stumbled and lunged, latching onto the tailgate. The truck grumbled to life. The engine purred, and Madison yelped excitedly, shifting into gear. "Go!" Zack shouted. "Hurry!"

Madison hit the accelerator, and the zombie flew off the back of the pickup as they swerved into the tunnel.

"That was a close one, huh?" Zack said to no one in particular.

"I just want my mom. . . ." NotGreg sobbed.

"Hate to break it to you, N.G." Rice yelled from up front. "But your mommy's a zombie." Greg frowned and burst into tears. "Hey, that rhymes."

"Shut up, Rice." Zack wobbled, balancing himself on the cargo bed with the truck's rough bounce.

The zombie moan disappeared as they reached a silver metal gate, which looked like the door of a spaceship.

"Great," Madison said. "All that for a dead end."

But she was wrong.

Behind the rearview mirror, a light ticked green. The tunnel vibrated and hummed. The metal gate lifted.

"E-Z Pass," Rice said. "Sweet."

Madison guided the pickup into the subterranean bunker as the gate lowered slowly behind them. Zack crouched down for balance and peered through the back window of the cabin. Inside the darkening tunnel, rapid spurts of gunfire crackled through the bunkered ceiling, like distant fireworks.

Just then, Twinkles licked Zack's face. "Thank you for saving me, Zachary!" Rice was doing the Twinkles voice again. "You're my all-time hero."

"Quit playing around, Rice," Zack said. "Do you hear those gunshots? It doesn't sound like they're messing around up there." Twinkles wriggled out of Rice's hands.

"Relax, dude. We made it. We got our secret formula. It's all good."

Zack glanced at Madison's leg. A splotch of red had soaked through the bandage. *The antidote,* Zack thought, *Madison's the medicine.*

The tires slowly rumbled on the grooved pavement, pushing the headlights' bright beam forward into the blackness.

Zack watched Madison as she primped herself in the rearview. She caught him staring in the mirror and stuck out her tongue, then twisted her face into a goofy sneer. She smiled.

Zack chuckled to himself and smiled back. But despite their discovery, he couldn't shake the feeling that this was not the end.

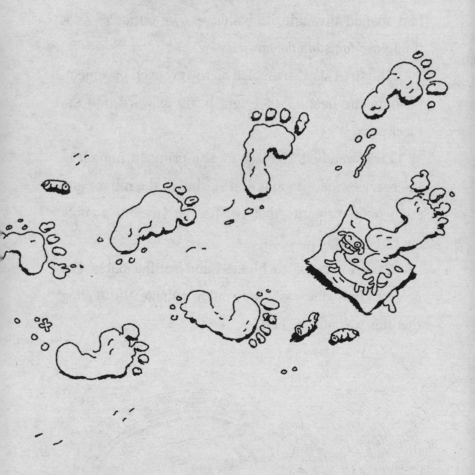

What brain-munching fiends will
the Zombie Chasers meet next?

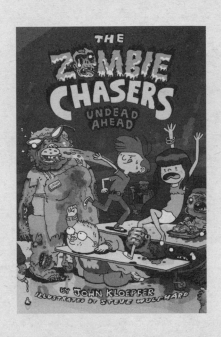

Turn the page for a sneak peek at
the next  novel,

CHAPTER

Zack Clarke stood up in the back of the pickup truck, his pulse still beating fast from the getaway. The halogen lights buzzed overhead as the truck drove into the flickering blackness of the subterranean bunker.

The zombie outbreak had erupted yesterday around suppertime, sweeping across the country in a matter of hours.

Now, cruising beneath the Tucson Air Force Base, Zack's sister, Zoe, was a zombie; his best friend and self-proclaimed zombie expert, Johnston Rice, had figured out the zombie antidote; Madison Miller, the most popular girl at Romero Middle School, was their only hope for survival; and Greg Bansal-Jones, their school's most feared bully, had turned into a whiny sissy after his own brief zombification, now insisting that he was *not* Greg.

NotGreg squirmed away from zombie Zoe, conked out in the cargo bed from the ginkgo biloba tranquilizer Rice had fed her a little less than an hour ago.

"Hey, man," NotGreg whimpered. "Will you untape me now?"

"Only if you keep quiet." Zack extracted the Swiss Army knife from his back pocket and clipped the duct tape from NotGreg's wrists. The un-bully closed an imaginary zipper over his mouth, then threw away a make-believe key.

I can't believe I used to be scared of this dude, Zack thought, and peered inside the truck's cabin. Fresh blood soaked through the gauze stretched around the bite-wound on Madison's leg, a present from zombie Greg. Rice was riding shotgun with Madison's Boggle puppy on his lap. Twinkles balanced his front paws on

2

the dashboard, seeming happy to be alive again after a stint as a zombie mutt.

"How's the leg?" Zack asked Madison.

"Okay, I guess," she said. "I'm gonna kill Greg, though."

"You mean NotGreg."

"Whatever."

"Ah," said Rice. "To Greg or not to Greg? That is the question."

"Shut up, nerd burger," Madison said wearily. "Nobody's talking to you."

Just then, Twinkles nudged Rice's backpack with his snout, sniffing at the rank specimen within the bag. Zack's stomach churned as he thought of the virus-carrying BurgerDog meat patty pulsating inside.

"Bow-wow," the puppy howled hungrily.

"Hey, slow down, Madison," Zack said through the slider window, and the truck rolled to a stop.

On their right, the tunnel opened up into a large room, split into two levels by a loading dock. Yellow biohazard barrels lined the base of the high cement walls. A thick

3

red splotch of zombie muck stained the square metal drain-grate in the center of the floor. The gory blotch extended into a curved smear that resembled a lowercase *j*. Uneven footprints were tracked around the ruddy trail of slime, as if the zombies had risen from a crawl.

The whole place reeked with the thick musk of disease, and Zack plugged his nose. Something was definitely rotten in Tucson.

"Eeeeee!" All of a sudden NotGreg let out a high-pitched squeal, grasping Zack's lower calf.

Zack whipped his head around.

A zombified soldier hung off the back of the truck, climbing up the tailgate. The undead commando stretched its zombie yap, cobwebbed with spittle, wide open. It growled and gargled, wriggling its rabid tongue.

"Step on it, Madison!" Zack ordered.

Just then, two more zombie soldiers scaled the sides of the truck, tumbling into the cargo bed with Zack and NotGreg. Their crooked limbs were set at impossible angles, as if they were half-squashed daddy longlegs.

The pickup shot forward, full-throttle.

"Zack!" Rice called from inside the cab, and handed off a metal crowbar. "Use this!"

Zack flung the piece of iron at the zombie soldier, striking him between the empty sockets of his eyes. The tailgate fell open, and the eyeball-less madman dropped with a splat into the receding tunnel.

"*Blaahrrgh!*" the other two zombies bellowed.

Zack felt around frantically on the rumbling cargo bed for another weapon and found the wooden base of his Louisville Slugger.

Across the flatbed, one of the zombies crawled on dislocated kneecaps toward NotGreg. The terrified un-bully cowered in the corner by the open tailgate, his arms curled up like a Tyrannosaurus rex's.

But Zack had his own problems.

The other zombie wheezed and tripped forward, falling full-force on top of him. In a flash, Zack flipped the bat horizontal, his ears pulsing hotly, as he strained to bench-press the zombie upward. Bulbous viral clusters curdled and bulged off the chin of the diseased sicko, and tusks of yellow-green phlegm hung from the corners of its raw swollen lips. The undead maniac grunted, and Zack felt his shoulder about to give. A ruptured infection dribbled off the zombie's cheek and onto the corner of Zack's mouth.

Puhtooey!

Zack heaved with every ounce of strength he had, and the slobbering beast was flung back, staggering to regain its balance. Zack stood, holding the Slugger tight, ready to strike.

Suddenly, Madison shrieked at the top of her lungs, and the pickup lurched to a vicious halt.

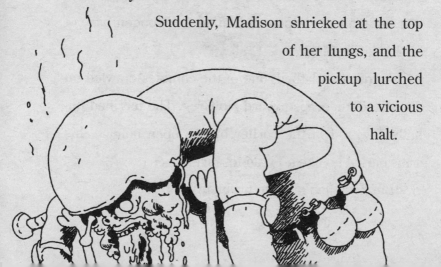

Zack flew backward and bashed his head on the truck bed with a hard *thunk*.

"Dang, Madison!" Rice said inside the cab. "What'd you stop for?"

"Didn't you see?" she asked. "That person just jumped right out in front of us!"

"Zombies aren't people, Madison."

"It wasn't a zombie, dork brain . . . it was some little soldier-dude!"

Zack slumped down to a seated position, his ears ringing from the impact. His vision blurred and his head flopped sideways. He was looking directly at his zombi-fied sister, Zoe. Her rolled-back, pupil-less eyes stared at him from behind the black metal cage of her face mask.

And just like that, as if fingers had snapped, Zack's mind went blank.

Want to read the rest of UNDEAD AHEAD?

Find out more at thezombiechasers.com

ACKNOWLEDGMENTS

This book would not have been possible without the contributions of the following people: Sara Shandler, Josh Bank, Katie Schwartz, and the creative and editorial staff of Alloy Entertainment and Elise Howard and Rachel Abrams of HarperCollins Publishers.

I would also like to thank my mother and father as well as the rest of my family and friends, in particular the Hahn family for their love and support throughout this project.

—J. K.